HUGH ZACHARY W … own
name and a variety o … Hughes and Evan
Innes, he wrote seve … novels in various genres, including horror, science fiction, and Westerns, most of them published as mass market paperback originals. He served in the U. S. Army and worked in broadcast journalism in Florida before commencing a career as a full-time writer in 1963. He once described himself as "the most published, underpaid and most unknown writer in the U. S." Zachary died in 2006.

WILL ERRICKSON is a lifelong horror enthusiast and author of the *Too Much Horror Fiction* blog, where he rediscovers forgotten titles and writers and celebrates the genre's resplendent cover art. With Grady Hendrix in 2017, he co-wrote the Bram Stoker Award-winning *Paperbacks from Hell*, which featured many books from his personal collection. Today Will resides in Portland, Oregon, with his wife Ashley and his ever-growing library of vintage horror paperbacks.

Cover: The cover reproduces the cover painting by George Ziel from the 1974 Fawcett paperback edition.

With a new introduction by
WILL ERRICKSON

VALANCOURT BOOKS

Dedication: For May, who planted the seed

Gwen, in Green by Hugh Zachary
Originally published by Fawcett Books in 1974

Published by Valancourt Books, Richmond, Virginia
http: / / www.valancourtbooks.com

ISBN 978-1-954321-55-7 (*paperback*)
Also available as an electronic book.

Cover painting by George Ziel
Cover text design by M. S. Corley

Set in Dante MT

INTRODUCTION*

Even to diehard readers of the obscure and the forgotten, the name Hugh Zachary will mean little. Perhaps it's because he used so many pseudonyms, like many a prolific author; or perhaps because he never really wrote that one great novel—jack of all, master of none. Despite his having written and published dozens of books in virtually all genres for decades, none of his works is in print today. Until, I am thrilled to say, now. His 1974 novel, *Gwen, in Green*, joins Valancourt's lauded reprint series of titles featured in my and Grady Hendrix's *Paperbacks from Hell*. For my money, Zachary's novel is almost a perfect example of its type, a paperback original featuring an eerie yet undeniably gorgeous cover illustration, complete with dated social mores, iffy sexual shenanigans, and a paranormal concept ripped right from a New Age pseudoscientific bestseller.

Born in 1928 in Ohio, Hugh Zachary wrote some in high school and spent his summers reading Edgar Rice Burroughs and working in a movie theater. Growing up while the romance of Hemingway and Fitzgerald still held sway, Zachary thought being a writer "would be neat," that it meant romance, money, and travel, not alcoholism, debt, and suicide. He served in the Army, attended college at University of North Carolina–Wilmington, then worked in radio and television for years, till the Sixties, when his struggle—after almost 300 rejections—to become a full-time professional writer finally paid off. *One Day in Hell*, his first novel, appeared in 1961, a low-rent cheapie paperback with cover art of a greasy, hairy-armed brute manhandling a scant-

* Hugh Zachary died in 2016. All quotes by him are from a 1998 interview with Sherman Hayes, University of North Carolina–Wilmington, Archives and Special Collections, and are used by permission. – W.E.

ily clad woman in a grimy-looking midnight wasteland. "It wasn't a bad book," he said years later on his webpage. "It was a terrible book."

For a while, Zachary wrote under the name Peter Kanto, publishing dozens of books for the erotic sleaze market, with not-quite-titillating titles like *A Man Called Sex*, *Make the Bride Blush*, *The World Where Sex Was Born*, *Moonlighting Wives*, and for no particular reason, my favorite, *The Girl with the Action*. Untangling his publication history seems a fool's errand, but Zachary—often helped in the writing of "intimate scenes" by his wife Elizabeth and the occasional bottle of grapefruit brandy—churned out paperback originals for various publishers into the Nineties. "I've written in every field except bestseller," Zachary quipped. Indeed: he and Elizabeth produced historical fiction, westerns, romance novels, sea adventures, Civil War tales, a post-apocalyptic series, even a regional cookbook, from his home on Oak Island, North Carolina.

Long a fan of the golden age of science fiction, he used the name Zach Hughes for more than a dozen books in the genre ("If you run into a book that you see 'Hugh Zachary' on, you know that I liked it"), beginning with *The Book of Rack the Healer* from Award Books in 1973. Most of what he wrote in the Eighties would be SF titles such as *Killbird*, *Sundrinker*, *Gold Star*, *Thunderworld*. Some of these books were nominated for the Nebula Award, which is given out by the Science Fiction and Fantasy Writers of America. Zachary mingled a bit with SF royalty: Theodore Sturgeon, Bradbury, up-and-comer Alan Dean Foster. (Not the mighty Asimov, however: "He was the 'King,' and he didn't have much time for the science-fiction world or for fans or anything else.")

Zachary may have been the only writer in existence to have a book fail because of the success of *Jaws*. In 1974, when he presented his publisher Putnam with *Tide*, about mutated fish, they loved it and were eager to make it into a bestseller—"Bestsellers are not written; they're made," Zachary noted—but then Peter Benchley's own monster fish story came out. Putnam changed their mind, telling Zachary there couldn't be two "marine peril" books on the bestseller list at the same time. *Tide* came out as a Berkley Medallion SF/thriller paperback a year later, marketed in the Michael Crichton mold, and "went down the drain."

He ventured into horror territory rarely, last with *The Revenant* (Onyx, 1988), complete with a banger of a cover adorned by a bloody, skeletal Confederate soldier. My horror cohort Grady Hendrix reviewed his 1981 paperback *Bloodrush* some five or six years ago for Tor.com; Grady notes it is "ostensibly a procedural mystery but that's dripping with so much blood and gore and weirdness that it crosses the line into straight-up horror." But it's 1974's *Gwen, in Green* that I am here to praise, a work of ecological terror and otherworldly mind control—and more than a smidgen of Seventies anything-goes sexiness.

Let's take a moment to appreciate that cover, from the brush of the incomparable George Ziel (written about at length in *Paperbacks from Hell*). Our Gwen is mesmerized by something beyond human ken, gazing in wild wonder, naked but perhaps not afraid, her hair held aloft by clinging vines. The luscious red of her lips and icy blue of her eyes stand in stark contrast to the sickly grey-green—a Ziel trademark—snippet of landscape. As she stands hip-deep in creeping flora and murky water, a white flower floats just below Gwen's belly button, an oh-so-demure symbol of fecund femininity. But what our lady of the swamp will bring is not life, but death, and plenty of it. Possessed by the spirit of some ineffable lifeforce, this young wife will wreak havoc on the men—always men—who rend the earth asunder in the name of electric power, quarterly gains, and golf courses.

Even the publisher should be noted: Gold Medal was established by Fawcett Publications out of Greenwich, Connecticut; the imprint hardly needs introduction to any vintage paperback collector. In 1949, Gold Medal began putting out mass-market paperbacks of original fiction—up till then, the format was almost solely used for reprints of hardcovers. Filled to the brim with action and thrills, disposable but satisfying two-fisted tales, these books upped the ante on the all-but-dead pulp clichés of yore. The early authors would become icons of popular fiction, in numerous genres: Jim Thompson, Louis L'Amour, Elmore Leonard, Richard Matheson, Robert Bloch, John D. MacDonald, even Kurt Vonnegut. The book designers knew that readers might not judge a book by its cover, but they'd certainly pay for one: with their immediate success, Gold Medal's paperback originals upended the entire publishing industry.

The impetus of the novel was the building of a power plant near Zachary's home on his beloved Oak Island. Bulldozers and constructions crews were all over "the most beautiful part of the island. The nicest trees and everything else; I'm not a 'tree hugger,' but . . . they were up there just tearing up the trees, right and left." Fusing this outrage with a bit of pseudoscience then popular from a bestseller called *The Secret Life of Plants*, as well as the zeitgeist of women's liberation and sexual empowerment, Zachary concocted a kind of revenge thriller against the encroachment of crass civilization on blissful nature.

Gwen and her husband, electrical engineer George Ferrier, both in their late twenties, have been married for seven years when the novel begins. Early chapters give the couple's background in North Carolina, their rocky start, their college years, their newlywed days. Gwen, whose childhood was one of neglect and misfortune, still feels shame from it: her widowed mother was a promiscuous woman who wasn't careful about keeping the bedroom door closed. A complex grew, encouraged by the teasing of Gwen's schoolmates, and so as an adult Gwen considers herself a prude, an uptight nut even—in the parlance of the era, frigid. But with George's eager ministrations, marital bliss (mostly) erases her past sexual hang-ups.

After coming into family money, George buys a plot of

undeveloped land on an island on the Cape Fear River; nearby a nuclear power plant is being built (George's research shows the danger of radioactivity is apparently nil). Now in come the developers, the earth movers, the bulldozers, and the crewmen to clear away the muck and brush and undergrowth and wild animals to build the Ferriers' new dream home. Gwen and George have terrific Seventies sex, sip gin-and-tonics looking out over their luscious landscape from their balcony while listening to records on their hi-fi. This is living!

Gwen is what I consider a comfort read: its isolated, forested setting is cozy, inviting, relaxing even. George works his land, swims every morning, the perfect picture of hale and hearty Seventies manhood. Gwen begins paintings of trees and caring for lush African violets, becomes enamored of the Venus fly-trap plants she finds at the nearby lake, starts feeding them raw hamburger. But creeping into this calm domesticity come her grotesque nightmares of pain, dismemberment, death: *"the mass roared down on her, huge teeth snapping at her. The mouth closed, clashing metal teeth, and she screamed once before she felt the tender flesh being punctured and rendered. Her upper body fell, being ripped from her legs and stomach and hips . . ."*

And things get worse: their dog dies mysteriously, the family cat attacks her, she has suicidal thoughts, and, oh yeah, she sleeps with the meter man. As Gwen begins to suffer fugue states, these dalliances get more graphic, more illicit, more, shall we say, neighborly. Sex, and a connection to the rich, lush earth itself, are the only things that take away the pain of her nightmares.

When she tells her husband of her bizarre, morbid, aching dreams he chides her, *"You are one spooky broad."* Gwen gets thee to a psychiatrist, Dr. Irving King, who's in his 80s and one nap away from retiring, and he says to her, *"You are much too pretty to be eaten by nightmare things."* (Paternalistic chauvinism is rarely absent from this era of paperback horror). But Dr. King turns out to be a kind of Van Helsing in the story, fascinated by Gwen's fugue states, her obsession with the flesh-eating Venus fly-traps—why, he's positive he once treated a similar case many years before . . .

It may not surprise you to hear that, occasionally, *Gwen* has some less-than-enlightened passages about gender, sexuality, and race. Pulpy popular fiction wasn't written to challenge the status quo; it was written for a mass audience, often an uncritical one, and sometimes it shows. *Gwen*'s momentary offenses seem mild and so dated that any experienced reader will know these words and ideas are the thoughts, musings, and words of characters that Zachary has created within various timeframes, and not the author's own views. I've certainly read more famous and more popular—and more recent—works that trade even more deeply in these uncomfortable notions.

Perhaps what endears the novel to me most is that, simply, it seems like Zachary had a good old time writing it: as he put it, he writes "as if I were watching a movie on a big screen. That's not really living it myself but watching it—observing it." The obvious pleasure he takes in his scenario, his confidence in his creation as he eases us into his tale, allows the reader to trust the author. Characters, even those who appear briefly, have specific natures and interior thoughts that ring true, all sketched out with a professional pen, and dialogue that, even at its crudest, sounds like it is sprung from people's mouths. The many "intimate moments," hinted at by the cover art, are delivered with aplomb, a wink, even when they veer ever so slightly into Penthouse Forum territory. In those days of *Deep Throat*, Xaviera Hollander's *Happy Hooker*, and Sylvia Kristel's *Emmanuelle*, *Gwen* is a natural fit. In other words, *Gwen, in Green* could only have been written in the early Seventies, and I'd have it no other way.

WILL ERRICKSON
September 2021

I

She knew about being ugly and unloved. The knowledge made her a soft touch for four-legged beggars and created a housing problem in a small development home of two bedrooms, one bath, combination kitchen and dining room, and a small living room. With the house a way-station for appealing strays, she skimped on grocery money to pay for mange treatments for a cowed mongrel pup and often passed up her own milk to nourish transient tomcats and the house regular, a great, black ex-tom named Satan. She hoarded every table scrap for the two outside dogs, Sam, a happy, funny part-Airedale, and Mandy, a doleful part-hound. In return, all animals loved her immediately, recognizing open, adoring gentleness, and the neighbors laughingly called her Marsha, the Enormous Mother. Although she was childless, her kitchen was open house for kids, with cookies always available on demand. Birds had a permanent feeding station in her back yard. Squirrels spoke to her by first name, barking from the oak trees, and took peanuts from her fingers.

So she was puzzled by the behavior of the ugly animal. His actions, she knew, were quite uncharacteristic.

George and the real estate salesman were ahead of her, pushing through dense second-growth brush to the bank of the tidal creek. On a by-path, she was threading her way along what seemed to be an animal trail when she came upon a small clearing where a mossy air plant had taken advantage of the sun to cover the ground. A dead, fallen longleaf pine showed its gray skeleton of resin-rich dead wood which, when split, burned torchlike and made excellent kindling for a fireplace. From the distant shore, across the wide marsh and the Intracoastal Waterway, heavy equipment growled like distant thunder, the low mumble-rumble coming and going on the shifting breeze. In the woods around her birds dug in the leaves and made a dry, crackling sound.

An opossum is a housecat-sized marsupial. What hair it has is dirty, gray, and always seems to be threatening to molt, to leave an even uglier creature, bald, graceless, vaguely repulsive. A needling snout contains a set of fifty sharp, tiny teeth, six more teeth than in the closest competing placental mammal, teeth which gnaw and tear at anything from insects to carrion, teeth which almost never threaten, however, except when shown in a hissing, cringing snarl when the animal is cornered.

"I won't hurt you, fella," Gwen said, in the voice she used to cajole squirms of delight from her adopted domestic pets.

The small, dirty, gray beast made a zigzagging advance, a few staggering steps to the right, a swaying movement to the left. Indirect as the course was, it closed the distance between them. In a sudden hush, she heard the hissing sound, saw saliva drip from the white, dead-meat mouth, opened wide.

The opossum is considered by many to be the leper of the animal world. Not by Gwen. She knew. She had empathy for any dumb beast.

But was she being menaced by this small, usually timid animal?

Perhaps she had stumbled near the animal's den and it was driven to unusual bravery to protect its home and its young. She looked around for a hollow tree, saw only low-growing brush and runted oaks. The area had been burned over not too many years past. Here and there a fallen log told of once proud, huge trees, but the new growth was young, weedy, dusty hot in the sun.

With awkward movements the opossum came closer, hissing wildly now, glaring at her with small, dull eyes. She backed off a few steps, saying softly, "All right, it's your turf, guy. I'm leaving."

To fend off a foolish, vague sense of threat, she laughed.

Brush closed around her as she left the clearing. The heat of the August afternoon seemed suddenly oppressive. Sweat beaded on her neck, ran down to dampen her blouse. George and the real estate man were out of hearing. She felt very much alone and very much ashamed to be frightened by a small, harmless animal, but a noise behind her caused her head to jerk around, sent a stiffening through her body. She turned casually and began to walk back along the twisting animal trail. The opossum began a lumbering run, overtaking her rapidly.

She left her pride behind. Low-hanging branches beat her face. Breathing hard, she veered off the trail and crashed through the brush. She slowed as she heard the voices of the two men, managed to look almost normal as she emerged from the brush onto the damp, black mud of the creek bank. Her slacks had a rip in the leg and there was a scratch on her cheek. George seemed not to notice her agitation. He had broken off a blade of marsh grass from the creek's edge and was chewing it thoughtfully. His coarse blond hair was mussed from walking through the woods. His shirt was darkened by perspiration. He stood with his legs apart. He was a stocky, masculine, handsome man, beautiful in Gwen's eyes. He winked a brown eye at her, chewed his blade of grass, kicked at a fallen log. She laughed, tensions relieved. Last week he had chewed a toothpick while kicking the tire of a new M.G. sportster. At her laugh, as if he knew, he grinned at her in that way he had and, as always, it made her feel warm and melty inside.

"So you know the situation," the real estate man was saying. "If it weren't for what those bastards"—he paused and looked quickly at Gwen—"are doing you couldn't touch this piece of land for a fraction of what we're asking."

A crackling in the brush behind her turned Gwen's head. The opossum had followed her. It came out onto the black mud and paused, swaying, hissing, dripping saliva.

"I'm not saying it will be quiet around here for the next couple of years," the real estate man said. "But if you know the problems and can accept them it's a helluva buy."

"No, Gwen," George said. "I absolutely refuse." It was an old joke between them. The real estate man looked at Gwen blankly, resenting her intrusion into his sales pitch. Gwen giggled nervously at the phrase, which was repeated each time she looked pityingly at a stray dog or cat.

The opossum surveyed them, hissed, advanced directly toward Gwen. She moved closer to her husband. "George?"

"Now you're not afraid of a little old 'possum," George said. "Not the fearless tamer of fierce, wild pussycats."

"Hey," the real estate man said, as the opossum continued to move hissingly toward Gwen's legs. He moved rapidly, seizing a hefty fallen limb.

"George," Gwen wailed, as the animal made a lunge which she avoided by skipping aside.

The real estate man put his shoulder into the blow, breaking the opossum's back. It struggled, feet and neck jerking. He hit it again and again until it was still. Then he poked it with his stick, turning it over. "Female," he said, as if that explained everything.

"Funny way for a 'possum to act," George said, his arm around a shivering Gwen.

"Rabid, probably," the real estate man said. "Had a couple of rabid foxes earlier."

Gwen shuddered. It was a terrible way to christen their new home site.

2

"George," she said sleepily, her breath hot on his neck, "now that you're rich, will you leave me for some pretty young girl?"

They were in George's lazy position, she sprawled atop, her breasts soft and hot against his chest. He liked to lie that way for a long time.

"Maybe I won't leave you," he said. "Maybe I'll just hire a hot-and-cold-running French maid."

"I'll kill you," she promised.

"You already have," he said, moving his loins. "No life at all left in the poor little beggar."

"Serves him right for being greedy," she said.

"You only complain afterwards," George said.

"That's bragging, not complaining," she said.

The room air conditioner activated its compressor with a whang and a bellow. In the new house there would be a central unit, quiet, efficient.

She tried to concentrate on the new house, envisioning its spacious rooms, trying to see in her mind the view from the balcony: dark, tidal Possum Creek and the wide, gray-green marsh.

It was not cool. Where their bare bodies made contact there was a slight stickiness, a damp feeling. Yet, feeling uncomfortable as the fires within her banked and the sex-induced amnesia faded, she reached for the sheet, pulled it over her legs and rounded rump. George sighed, but said nothing.

"It's sinful," she said.

"Humm."

"In bed in the afternoon," she said.

"Delightfully sinful," he said.

At least she could tease about it now. She had made progress in seven years of marriage.

George dozed. He made a funny little buzzing sound in his throat. She was alone. Softened, he was still inside her, but she was alone and, although she had come a long way to be able to lie thus, she still felt more at ease with the sheet over her. Underneath the light covering, body heat made for perspiration. And in her mind, underneath the comfortable blanket of her love for George, she felt the old shame grow.

"Don't think about it," she told herself.

She thought about it when she was alone or when she was lying with George after sex and he was off, away from her, resting, dozing. Then the change came over her and she felt her body dirty against his. Although she'd been winning the battle for years, the fight was not over. There comes a time in life when one has to accept oneself as one is, when it is no longer possible to fool oneself. There were times when she thought she'd won, finally, but then she would remember, or the old hurt would begin to pound like an abscessed tooth and she would hear his voice in her mind:

"Gwen, Jesus, you're all screwed up. Maybe you need help."

But she was not the one who had had an affair with Grace Dowling, shameless bitch that Grace was. She was not the one who had betrayed, and just ten months after both she and George had vowed eternal love.

In more controlled moments she considered George's affair with Grace to be the turning point; she could, almost, be grateful to Grace. At such moments, if she had been granted the ability to change the past she would have erased her mother. *Dele* her, as the crosswords said. Strike her out. Make her nothing more than a blank space in her mind.

"Gwen," she said to herself, "you worry too much."

That had to be true. If she were really a nut she would be able to scrap all the memories and be fashionably neurotic with the rest of the world. If anything, she was too sane. She couldn't even drink enough to forget what she was doing. When she got too high she invariably suffered the agonies of the damned and felt suicidal over some drunken, relatively innocent escapade. Not that she was a wild one. Not Gwen Ferrier. But she was a talker when she was drinking and she said things like, "Ruthie, there is a certain responsibility involved in having pets." Ruthie, a neighbor, had a nice, friendly beagle which was left outside in the coldest weather and which, in the fall, was always laden with huge, hulking, gray, sick, puky ticks. And Ruthie wouldn't be insulted, she'd just laugh, but next morning Gwen would remember and feel exposed, for she kept herself, mostly, giving of her inner thoughts only to George.

So if you remember things like that and let them fester inside you and make you feel as if you should run over to Ruthie's and apologize, how do you forget Mama?

"You don't try to forget her," George said. "You try to understand her. Gwen, she was a young woman. She had a bad break."

"But my father loved her so," Gwen would say. "I remember how he'd kiss her and tell her she was pretty."

"She was pretty," George said. "And sexy."

Yes, she was that.

After her father died they lived in an apartment in the nice section of Winston-Salem, if Winston-Salem can be said to have a nice section. It was a small apartment with one bedroom, a sitting room, and a kitchen with a dining alcove. Gwen's bed was a pull-out couch in the sitting room, next to the bedroom door and sometimes they forgot even to close the door. And it was always a different man and, as George put it, her mother was a noisy lay, panting, moaning, crying out.

"Your mother does it," the boys would say. "What's wrong with you?"

She was a skinny child with weak arches which pained her. The insurance money wasn't plentiful enough to buy clothing for her mother and two bottles of vodka a week and still have enough left over for the orthopedic shoes for Gwen. While not drinking or making love, her mother sewed, cutting down fancy party dresses for school clothing so that, in Gwen's mind, she always looked freaky.

"She was just a lonely broad," George would say. "Don't condemn her for wanting to get something out of life."

It took her a long time to learn that her mother wasn't in pain when she would cry out and sob-laugh at the same time. And everyone knew. The kids in school laughed at her, the dark-haired, skinny, rather homely little girl in the cut-down red party dress with the lace and frilly sleeves, the girl whose mother put out.

"George"—she wept as she said it one spring night when she was a sophomore in college at Chapel Hill—"I can't marry you."

"Why?"

"I can't, that's all."

He insisted. "All right," she said grimly. "If you must know. I'm frigid."

He laughed. "You'll have to prove it to me."

She'd known him for over a year. His smile and his ease of manner had lured her into rare dates with him, had worked on her until, although she told herself that she didn't love him, could never love a man, she looked forward to seeing him, saw him with a quick little flip of delight deep next to her heart, let him kiss her.

"You're a nice girl, Gwen," he told her. "The marrying kind."

She knew the flip words. Her affliction was a hidden thing. "Aren't you the hypocritical one? I've heard about you."

"Experience is important in a man," he said, grinning. "Women don't need experience. It's an instinctive act with them."

He was warm, obviously sensual, but he never tried to handle her, never forced her to indulge in the college ritual of making out. When he asked her to marry him, she'd never felt a male hand on her breast, had not even used Tampax, not able to bear even the thought of having a sanitary tube inserted into that virginal tract. Gwen the prude. Gwen the nut.

So she told him and he listened. "I wouldn't be good for you," she concluded. "You deserve a warm, exciting woman. Not me. You can have any girl you want. Why me?"

That grin. "I always promised my mother I'd marry a good girl, and you're the only virgin in North Carolina above three years old."

"Gee," she said flippantly, "what a solid foundation for a marriage."

She refused to see him for months. When the year was ending, he cracked up his motorcycle coming up the hill from Durham, whammed into a series of pine trees, demolished the bike, lay in the hospital with a severe concussion.

"God, Gwen," he said, seeing her there when he regained consciousness, "I feel like a seven-acre boil."

"You're Gwen," his mother said. "We've heard so much about you. And I'm so pleased you've come. George was asking for you while he was delirious."

Asking for her.

When he was ambulant, they drove in a borrowed car to Raleigh, checked in nervously at a Holiday Inn. "I won't marry you," she told him, bleeding inside but making the sacrifice, "but I will show you why."

He thought a drink would relax her. But when he undressed her, she felt as if her body were made of steel and ice. His hands caused her to cringe. He was kind, patient, gentle. His heated breathing made her hate him, made him the embodiment of all that long parade of faceless men who breathed and grunted and wallowed with her mother. She lay stiff as oak, suffering his hands, his kisses.

"We'll stop," he said.

"No," she said, tears running down her cheeks. "I have to prove to you."

"Why?"

"Because I love you and I want you to understand."

"Can't you relax?"

"Yes."

She was limp. She did not cry out when he penetrated her. She was dry and it was painful. She was pleased that it hurt her so. She wanted to be punished, for she was hurting him, too. He loved her, wanted her. And she had nothing to give—nothing, that is, which would compensate him for devoting his life to her. She lay limply as he worked in her and he stopped.

"Don't you feel anything?"

"I feel dirty," she said cruelly.

"God," he said, stopping his movement. He lay there for a long time. He talked to her, told her she was beautiful. She was not. She had mouse-brown hair which was fine as baby hair and completely unmanageable. She had a nose too long for her face. Her skin was mottled by dark, frecklelike blemishes. Had they been freckles, they would have been cutely attractive, but as blemishes they were just disfiguring. She was small-breasted. Her thighs did not meet, giving her a bow-legged look as she stood before her mirror naked. Her ankles, because of her weak arches, tended to touch, her feet splaying outward. Her two front teeth showed a large gap. No, she was not beautiful.

"You have a great ass," he said. "And I love your titties."

She was sick with shame, feverish with disgust.

"We could work on it," he said. "It's normal, Gwen, sex is."

"I know. I'm not normal, though."

"Does it make any difference that I love you, that I want to help you?"

Apparently it did. His patience, his gentleness, paid off. Not the first time. The first time his youthful eagerness pushed him over the brink and she felt his seminal fluid rush into her. She felt nauseous, hating his sweating body, his gasping breathing, his clinging.

"You see," she said, "as I told you, I feel nothing. Do you believe me now?"

"A lot of girls don't enjoy it the first time," he said.

"I hated it, George," she said. "That's the difference."

"Did you hate me?"

"Yes, when you were . . . doing it."

"I see."

"So you see that it would be a mistake."

"Would you let me try again?"

She wanted to bathe his sweat from her, wanted to be away from him, away so that she could rid herself of his filthy sperm, wash his taste from her mouth. But he was so concerned, so hurt. She allowed him to make love to her. He did vile things. First he cleaned her with a cloth from the bathroom, then he did a thing so sickening that she almost made him stop. Only her desire not to hurt him more, to convince him that marriage was impossible, stopped her from bolting.

"Nothing?" He had a moustache. He was revolting. She was crying quietly. To hide it from him, she bent up, pulled the sheet over his crouching body, hid his head and shoulders and face beneath it. Then she could pretend it wasn't happening. He was a warm-wet feeling there, that was all. She closed her eyes. It was growing dark outside. It went on and on and she was able to divorce herself from the act.

She lay in total darkness, limply submitting to his touch, his obscene kiss, his fast, labored breathing. And her clitoris swelled. A tendril of something went shooting down, down, centered there. She jerked her eyes open, shocked. Darkness, the sheet over him. A stiffening in her legs, an almost imperceptible lifting of her loins. She recognized her feeling. She'd known it in her dreams. A wild hope sprang up in her. He, feeling his love-making bear fruit, redoubled his efforts. His tongue was a living entity. With a gasp, she pulled the sheet up, up, covered her head, hid herself from herself and from the world, tucked the sheet under her head and lowered her hands to pull on his shoulders, his head. He came to her, filled her, and there, in darkness, hidden by the covering sheet, air getting stale with their joint gasps, she found that certain body movements are instinctive.

She giggled wildly, happily. George kissed her, smeared his musky smell over her cheeks.

"See?" he asked.

She did not tell him that her first ecstasy had been a brief moment followed by sickening remorse, self-hate, shame. She had hope and she loved him.

In all her life she had never had anyone to love her and her alone. In all her life, till George, she had never had anyone.

In order for her to keep her scholarship, they were married in secret. She was just twenty. He was almost twenty-two. She lived in the girl's dorm, he in a fraternity house. On weekends, when he had the money, they would drive to the Raleigh area motels. There they would hide beneath the sheets in darkness until her shame and disgust was overcome by her body.

Ten months after they were married, George had sex in the back seat of his car with vivacious, blond Grace Dowling. Had he been content with having Grace only once, Gwen would never have known. But he was greedy. Greedy George. On an ensuing occasion George and Grace parked behind the stadium and were surprised by the campus patrolman, a talkative fellow. The policeman let it be known that he had caught Grace Dowling, the blond cheerleader, the one with the great legs, with her flimsies down. The name of the boy was almost incidental to the story, but it was mentioned and the story got around to Gwen. Confronted, George confessed.

Ten months after they were married.

She would not see him. She withdrew into herself and accepted as a fact a suspicion she'd had all along. She was not enough woman for George. Her hang-ups were just too much. She could never make him happy. In all of her life, till George, she had had no one. Now she had no one again.

The reconciliation was brought about by George's parents. Confused, hurt, guilty, George talked to his father, who then talked to his mother. Mrs. Ferrier, a handsome, kindly woman, talked with Gwen in Gwen's room.

"If only you had not kept the marriage secret, darling," Mrs. Ferrier said. "If only we'd known."

Woman to woman, Mrs. Ferrier said, how foolish to live apart. Naturally a man would fall victim to the first loose girl who came along. Men, she explained, are weak creatures in some ways, lacking in resistance to the wiles of predatory women. It had happened, she insisted, simply because those two foolish children would not announce their marriage and live together as man and wife should. That, she announced, was the way it would be. There would be an immediate change. Gwen was not to worry about a foolish scholarship. The Ferriers would pay her expenses, would rent them a cottage. They were not wealthy people, but they had enough to help their son's happiness.

"But I'm inadequate," she said.

"Nonsense," said her mother-in-law. "You just need counseling, that's all."

"Gwen, you need help."

Under the sheets in the summer. Under the blankets in the winter. Cringing when she had to undress in front of him, hating it, loathing her body, feeling dirty. But, helpless hypocrite that she was, enjoying it once it was done.

3

Possum Creek had a tidal variation of some four feet. When the tide was full, it lost some of its muddy, black look and showed a tinge of the green ocean water which fed it. Falling, the tide carried debris from the vast marshes on the inland side of the island. The creek abounded in blue crabs in season, was dimpled with the jumps of popping mullet, had once, before upstream pollution, been a prime speckled-trout fishing ground. The creek meandered up from the Cape Fear alongside the northern end of Pine Tree Island, sweeping out in a *U* to eat into the marsh, coming back to lick the land and leave bare, black mud banks under the spreading branches of huge pines.

The island itself was a long one. In past years the Ferrier family had summered in a cottage on Big Hill Beach, a sprawling resort community which occupied the southern end of the island. Thus, George was familiar with the locality and had spent some of his boyhood exploring the creeks of the marshes in a small boat, trudging through the undeveloped woodlands at the northern end, digging for pirate gold, and doing all the other things young boys do when left to their own devices in an outdoor setting with plenty of salt water.

Upon graduation, George brought Gwen to Big Hill, covered her with musty-smelling sheets in the family cottage, and did what she'd come to believe he liked doing best. They had been married just over two years and he had a job lined up in Winston with the family firm. During the month spent on the beach, he escorted her to the places of his boyhood, including the point at the northern end.

She questioned the sudden transition from resort development to woodlands. George had coaxed a rusting jeep into operation, and they pushed through little-traveled logging roads to the point. There she saw the foundation ruins of what must have been a huge house. It had obviously burned down. Charred pieces of wood stuck up in exposed sandy spots.

"Old boy from New Jersey owns the whole end of the island," George said. "This was his house. It burned before I was old enough to take advantage."

"Of what?" she asked innocently.

George grinned lewdly. "They still talk about her. She was much younger. A real hot one. They still talk, some of the old boys, about how all they had to do was sneak through the woods, whistle, and she'd come out."

"All men," Gwen said, "are horrible."

"Honey, it always takes two."

She didn't want to discuss it.

"Didn't make any difference what age or how many. There was a little gazebo down by the clear pond. That's where they'd go, with the old boy up in the house playing with his stamp collection or something."

"George," she said. "Please."

The clear pond was an oddity. It was ovate, had the bright green color of the water holes left after a massive strip-mining operation for phosphates, held no life other than plant life, and owned its own grisly tradition. Once it had been a favorite spot for swimming, until a young couple, after the house had burned, had driven their car to the site and swam nude. Their car was discovered a full day later and their bodies a few hours after that, nude, close together, the girl's arms still locked around the boy, her hair streaming upward in the clear, green water, her eyes wide, wild.

Gwen refused on their honeymoon, after their graduation, to go into the water. George stripped, ran into the water, blew and puffed and swam the hundred-yard length of the pond, yelled, "The water's great, honey," and came out dripping to laugh at her.

"What I want," he said, brushing clinging drops from his skin so that he could dry in the hot sun, "is to own this point, every acre of it. Then I'll build a house with the bedroom out on pilings or cantilevered out over the pond. There'll be a little balcony outside the bedroom and each morning I'll just walk out, fall into the water and then I'll never have to take a bath, except in the winter time when the pond freezes over."

At the time, neither of them dreamed that his talk was more than idle chatter.

Death and a good insurance man made it possible. Back in Winston-Salem, George went to work with his father. His fresh degree in electrical engineering made it possible for him to pass the F.C.C. test for a First Class Radio-telephone ticket. With this piece of paper from the federal government, he was allowed to repair licensed communications equipment, adding a new dimension to his father's business. In a time when citizen's band radio was becoming a fad, George was kept busy, but he took time to learn the other aspects of the business, and when he'd been there a year he was made a full partner. His draw, plus end-of-the-year bonuses, made life comfortable for them, but they were not rich until a small commercial airliner crashed coming into a Virginia mountain town, killing, along with a dozen others, George's mother and father. There was partnership insurance, mortgage insurance, life insurance, two rather hefty travel policies purchased at a vending machine before the elder Ferriers left for their holiday in New York, and a couple of gimmick accident policies which also paid off. George, at twenty-seven, found himself the sole owner of a thriving television and appliance store and, after taxes, holding cash which, when the proceeds of the sale of the store were added, came to just over three hundred thousand dollars.

Gwen understood. "Honey," he said, "when I walk into that place I look around for Dad. I expect him to pop up from the rear and say, 'Hey, boy, we aren't running a bank, you're due here at ten of nine sharp'; or, 'Hey, boy, it's your turn to sweep up.' It's damned lonely, honey. I don't think I can take it. All the fun's gone out of it."

"We can't live the rest of our lives on it," practical Gwen said.

"No. I can make a dollar. Dad saw to it that I had a little business experience crammed into my head. He didn't let me spend all my time back at the workbench. I could find a new town, maybe one of the developing areas along the coast. I could start small and just concentrate on repair work. I like that. I'd never want to give up playing with electronic junk. It's just that, well, it's not the same at the store."

So they sold the store and bought the new M.G. and, to take George's mind off the death of his parents, drove to Florida with the top down. They swam in a clear, cold spring in a national forest near Ocala, where George was reminded of the green, strange little pond on Pine Tree Island.

The area, they found, was changing rapidly. A large electric company had started construction of a multiple nuclear generating plant. In a backward county, where tourism and fishing were the chief industries, the nuclear plant was welcomed, at least by those who owned land and stood to gain by increased land values, and by businessmen and booster types in general. The plant was located near the village of Ocean City, on the Cape Fear. A canal would draw Cape Fear water to the plant to cool the reactors and would extend, in a huge, wide scar, across a natural marsh along a creek on the inland side of the Intra-coastal Waterway, go under the Waterway in huge pipes, rise again to cut straight across a producing marsh to Pine Tree Island, and there take a big bite through the end of the undeveloped property next to the point. It would be, the environmentalists said, the last cooling canal built in the United States. Cooling towers cost more money, and, naturally, the power company first filed for permission for the less expensive cooling canal. There were no voices in the county strong enough to stop the despoliation of a good swath of swamp and producing marshland.

When George and Gwen drove to the island they stopped in to talk with a real estate man, an aging fellow who had watched the beach grow from nothing, be destroyed in a killer hurricane, then come back to be an instant slum with cheaply built waterfront cottages, dinky second-row houses and other weekend retreats scattered about the woodlands.

"We might just be able to work something out," the real estate man said when George expressed his interest in the point property. "The canal is taking a big bite of it. The rest will be on the other side of the canal, sort of an island in itself. The old boy that owned it is dead and his heirs seem to be pretty well off up there in New Jersey somewhere. They sent a lawyer down to dicker with the power people and got the going price for undeveloped land out in the middle of the county. They didn't even seem to know that waterfront and creek front is worth a dollar."

George rented a cottage and waited nervously while the real estate man contacted the lawyer who had represented the absentee owners of the point. "I told him," he said to George and Gwen, "that the place was killed as far as development is concerned. No one in his right mind is gonna build a nice house next door to a canal full of radioactivity."

"Just George," Gwen said.

"Actually," the old man said, "there ain't much radioactivity in it."

"I know," George said. He'd made quite a study of the situation, getting his hands on the power company's reports, talking to anyone who had either information or gossip to offer. "The radioactive level of the water will be less than that of the background radiation."

To Gwen, this meant that even if it were less than normal background radiation, it was still an additional amount of radiation. However, her seven years with George had been the happiest time of her life. At last she had someone who loved her for herself. This was surely worth more than exposure to a minute amount of radiation. She'd have braved the Van Allen belts in a bikini for George. If it turned George on, it was fine with her.

Two hundred three and a quarter acres were involved. The lawyer asked seven hundred per acre. George winced. The real estate man, with George in attendance on an extension telephone, snorted. "We're not even close enough to talk," he said.

The real estate man offered one hundred per acre, following his offer with a detailed run-down of the disadvantages of the property. Some of it was low, there was no timber, just second-growth stuff, and it was going to be cut off from the island by the canal. But he had told George earlier that the power company would have to build a bridge over the canal to give access to the property.

"If the terms are favorable," said the lawyer, "we might come down to five hundred."

"How about cash at three hundred?" the real estate man asked. "That's our first, last and firm offer. Take it or get stuck with a swamp cut off from the roads by a radioactive hot water canal."

They took it. George whistled as he tried to crowd the amount into the small allotted space on the check. Sixty-one thousand twenty dollars and no cents. Gwen felt weak. She had worried about money most of her life. To her, writing a check for the amount of the new M.G. was pure extravagance. Now George was laying out over sixty thousand dollars for a swamp cut off from the roads by a hot water radioactive canal. Whee, she thought.

"Don't worry," George said. "We'll have it all paid for. The house will be paid for. Our taxes will be low, because we'll be assessed for undeveloped land. We won't have to touch the rest of the money once we're established. I'll make enough working part-time to live on. We don't have any expensive habits like shooting heroin or wearing French originals."

"I might like to wear French originals," she said.

"Look, honey, if that's what you want I'll tear up the check."

"If you're laying out too much in a lump, young fella," said the real estate man, "I'd be willing to take some of the waterfront off your hands."

"What do you want?" George asked, being very, very serious.

"You know, silly," she said. "I want what you want."

"Not here in front of the nice man," he grinned.

Crazy, delightfully crazy, and so damned pretty she could charge herself up just by looking at that shock of stubborn, wild blond hair.

Then there was the architect's fee. And bulldozers to cut a road which wouldn't tear up the new M.G. And the sound of heavy equipment twenty-four hours a day. The power company was attacking the canal from both ends, eating the woodland on the inland side in vast gulps, and sending a huge, floating drag line to the ocean side to start cutting a trench through the dunes, chewing up into the land, exposing the dead and water-logged roots of an ancient cypress forest. Bulldozers. Drag lines. Earth movers. Whoom. Crash. Creak. Rumble.

"I'm going to watch it go up stick by stick," George said. "How would you like to buy a mobile home and put it next to the clear pond, and that way we'll be there to supervise every nail?"

In the end, he compromised. They rented a small, dark, damp little house built of cement block and cheap, varnished interior paneling. It was a gloomy dungeon and they spent as little time in it as possible. They saw every movie which came to Ocean City and the nearby, larger town. They took short trips to the Outer Banks, to the mountains, to Charleston. The money spent in this manner seemed insignificant when compared with the weekly bills for material and labor as the contractor began work on the dream house on Possum Creek.

When the time came, Gwen actually enjoyed shopping for appliances, light fixtures, carpeting, and all the little goodies which were going into the dream house. She found a magnificent old chandelier in a junk shop. George rewired it. She spent long, dusty, hot, exciting days prowling antique shops, bought marbled-topped furniture, good, sturdy chairs made in 1948, much more comfortable than anything on the market in the new furniture stores. And cheaper, even when reupholstered in good quality crushed velvet.

"Look," George said, "if you're gonna make the house look like a Victorian harem, let's have a red rug."

If George wanted a red rug, George got a red rug. She built the big, glass-fronted room around it, and made the walls gleaming white, the fireplace antique brick, the furniture warm in velvet and gold and rich blue.

"Gaudy," she said, "but sort of nice."

"I can hardly wait to try out the rug," George said, grinning his teasing, sensual grin.

Watching a large house being constructed is, in many ways, a frustrating experience. At first, when there is just the foundation, it looks as if one has miscalculated and has decided to build too small. Then, with the floor studs in place and the sub-flooring down, making the house a huge platform, it begins to look large enough to land helicopters. It shrinks when the wall studs go up, and becomes dark and gloomy when the roof and walls are in place. During all this time, the progress is daily. A trip upstate brought surprises on returning, for the workmen would have done something fantastic like closing in the whole airy structure with black weatherboard. The brick and stone work went rapidly, too, and then things slowed to a frustrating crawl as the interior finish began.

But one can get to know a house during construction. George and Gwen had a routine. Breakfast, when they waked naturally, a drive to the house site to see who was working, a day spent in idle, happy activity, and then a trip back through the woodlands in the late evening, with the sun low and the second-growth denseness becoming dark and forbidding. They'd walk through the house and discuss progress. George would walk around it, admiring it. As it took shape, he was more than pleased.

It was an attractive house. Long, low, it had multiple roof lines, lots of glass, stone for accent, brick for color, and stained wood for texture. The bedroom end of the house snuggled next to the sandy shore of the clear pond. George was endlessly anxious to see the balcony added, but the contractor saved it for last.

It was growing chill. The rented house had poor heat, just baseboard electric units which, when turned on, promptly blew a fuse. Fortunately, the weather held. November was a glory, nights cool and making for good cuddling in bed, but the days were pure Indian Summer. The rains were less frequent than usual, allowing for full-time work. Gwen began moving her furniture in in early December. The rural electric cooperative had run a line along the old right of way; a line had once extended up the point to the burned house, which had stood just a few hundred yards away from the new building. The house was heated now. It was lighted. It was cozy and huge and empty, and one evening, before the moving began, while there was nothing in the house but huge expanses of red carpet, George gathered fat pine kindling and wood and built a fire. "I christen thee George's House of Lust," he grinned, bumping beers with Gwen before attacking her playfully and rolling her in front of the roaring fire on the thick, red carpet. She fought playfully, but gave in, her feeling for him overflowing. At first, she was uncomfortable, felt the old shame and dirt as he exposed her, growing more intense, but still growling playfully as he removed her slacks and panties, undid her bra, pushed it up under her neck.

The floor was hard. She kept thinking that someone would walk up. Every light in the house was on. There were large expanses of glass. She kept turning her head to look at the black glass and the darkness beyond and didn't achieve. George did. Then he prowled, bare, over the house, drinking beer and admiring the barren beauty of the rooms. She envied him. He was the original model for a happy fellow, no worries, no hang-ups, just a heart very easily made glad. Since she had the same things, plus George himself, why couldn't she loosen up, enjoy his ribald, happy sex, and forget everything but the new house, George, and her luck?

George didn't want any lawn to mow. The contractor sent in a crew, picked up the building debris, smoothed the earth, and left it natural. Falling leaves covered the bare areas, making it look as if the house had been there not just weeks but years. And George had his balcony. It was built on two pre-stressed concrete pillars which had been sunk into the very edge of the clear pond. The balcony extended out some twenty feet, riding on huge cypress beams. It was six feet above the water and reached to the quickly shelving depths of the pond. It made an excellent diving platform. Below it, to shore up the bank of the pond, there was a brick patio on a concrete slab with an outdoor grill.

In the house there were two bedrooms, one of them behind the balcony and huge, the other suitable for guests and, in the future, for a nursery. There were three baths, one in each bedroom and one in the big playroom, which housed a pool table, a ping-pong table, a dart game, a poker table, and a stereo set for parties. There was a large room for George's personal use, and a room with northern glass exposure which was, temporarily, a TV room, but which could be converted into a studio if Gwen ever got serious enough about her hobby of painting to want such a work area. There was a combination kitchen-dining room, separated by dark, beautifully rubbed cabinets, and a very large main room with its glass wall looking toward the marsh, which was visible only through chinks in the solid growth of trees. Then there were storage areas, an appliance room, a closed garage, and cypress decks off the front.

Approaching the house was always an experience for Gwen. The woodland had not been disturbed, save for widening the old timber road. Then, suddenly, stone and stained wood and glass and brick appeared in tantalizing flashes through the trees, and then one was in the circular drive, and it was breathtaking. She loved it. She felt very warm toward it. She'd watched it grow from bare bones, she knew every piece of wood in it, and she felt so much at home in it that she would walk the length of the house, in darkness, without so much as a tremor.

This seemed important to her. The basic insecurity of her childhood had marked her in many ways. One of them was in her habit of wanting a night-light. She'd always slept with a light. It was just the way she was. And she locked doors and windows. She also, when feeling low, looked under beds and into closets before retiring, even with George in the house. If she didn't look under the bed she couldn't turn to snuggle with George, thus putting her back to the side of the bed and exposing it to that something which would reach up something, a bony claw, an unidentified thing, and dig into her back, digging, digging, cutting the tender flesh there and making her scream with agony. And a trip in darkness through the rooms of the dark little rental house would have been unthinkable. Some*thing* could lurk in each shadow.

Her insecurity had been a topic for many deep discussions during the seven years of their marriage. George had grown to accept it, to try to ignore it, since he couldn't cure it.

"What do you expect to find under there?" he'd ask as she knelt to look under the bed before turning off the light.

"I don't know," she would say truthfully. "Nothing, I guess."

"Your lover?"

"Silly."

"Let us explore the nature of fear," George would say, in his early attempts to cure Gwen. "Basically, it is the fear of death which is underneath all fear. Once you had another fear, the fear of losing your chastity by force, but that is no longer possible, so that fear must not be what makes you look under the bed."

"I'm not expecting to discover a mad rapist," she said.

"We fear dead bodies," he said. "We shudder at tales of walking dead and rotting bones coming to life, and we scream if we find a severed hand in bed with us."

"You're pretty terrible, you know?"

"What do we see when we see the severed hand? We see ourselves. We are reminded by the sight of a dismembered body that we, too, can be dismembered. Ergo, we are fearing death. Honey, we're all going to pop off. You could trip over the vacuum cleaner and break your neck. You could choke to death on a potato chip. You could eat something that made you sick and rupture an artery or something by the force of your vomiting and die of peritonitis before I could get you to a hospital."

"I don't know, George. It's silly, I know. It's not a person. Really. I know the human animal is capable of great violence against his fellows, but I don't shudder thinking about an evil *man* or something."

"Being afraid of the dark is something most people outgrow. I pulled that night-light bit when I was a kid, and my dad took me out into the woods coon hunting one night and left me to guard the fire. I saw wolves and bears in every shadow. Then, after a while, when they didn't eat me, I got brave and started throwing sticks at them. The cowardly bastards ran away. They were more scared than I. Now I could understand if you saw wolves and bears under the bed, then you could throw shoes at them and run them away."

"Just let me work it out, huh?" she asked.

"We fear pain. Now I, myself, brave stud that I am, can get the shudders thinking of torture. Remember the John D. MacDonald book where the evil guys were torturing someone? He said, and I agree, that torture is bad, but relatively ineffective unless you know, deep in your heart, that the cat doing the torturing is a real nut. I mean, you can have a cigarette thrust into your bare titty and it'll hurt like hell and you'll scream, but you know that it'll heal. Same with splinters under the fingernails. They'll come out, even if you have to cut off the nail. Even the nail will grow back. But if you know that this cat is going to do something irreparable to you, like cut off an arm or gouge out an eye, then you know real fear. The fear of dismemberment and death. Now since you don't have to worry about that, unless I eat loco weed and go ape, then what do you fear?"

"I don't know."

"The dark? I should take you coon hunting."

"I'd hang onto you with both hands."

"Not a bad idea," he said. "Grab me now."

But there was no fear in the dream house. Working hard, hair in a scarf, muscles aching, she arranged and moved furniture and settled in and slept deep sleep the first full night. George, up before her, was whistling and happy. "You left the door unlocked all night and no one ate us," he said.

She hadn't even thought about checking the doors. And she could walk the length of the house. She did this several nights later, waking with a thirst and going all the way to the kitchen for ice water, neglecting to turn on the lights because she hadn't bothered to put on anything over her pajama top. "Well, Gwen," she said. "Well."

Such a friendly house it was. Warm. The colors were vibrant and everything was so clean and new. It was a glorious winter. George had rented a building in Ocean City and was installing equipment. He had plenty of work, more than he wanted, actually. Ocean City was a fishing town and there were dozens of boats with radiotelephones. He was the only man within thirty miles licensed to work on them. He was swamped with radio work and depth-recorder repair, and he had to turn away quick, easy money doing home TV sets. They were no longer living on their capital. Their expenses were low. They ate what they liked, drank the best booze, went to movies, and had dinner at nice places, and still there was more money coming in than going out and life was a blast, with a fire in the fireplace and Don Ellis playing "Turkish Bath" on the magnificent music system George had installed in the big room, and the wind whistling outside and a light snow in February to give a fairyland atmosphere to their woods.

Inland, the snow brought hardship and death. It was a heavy fall, closing schools and roads and bringing the entire state to a frozen standstill. Even in Ocean County schools closed, but there, near the warmer water, the effects were short-lived. Early morning was elves' work on the trees, whose limbs were artistically draped in snow and diamonded with ice. George, the early riser, rolled her out and forced her to walk, still half asleep, to the glass doors leading onto the balcony. She was jarred into full alertness by the beauty. The white glare squinted her eyes and tears formed, tears of joy engendered by beauty.

She put on a set of George's insulated hunting underwear and rounded her form with layers of outside clothing. He met her outside, having gone out before her to track the clean, virgin snow. Playful snowballs flew. There was a thin film of ice on the clear pond, making it a glassed-in jewel of green.

Before the snow began to melt at mid-morning, they had covered the estate. They both said the word "estate" in quotation marks, teasing each other about having satisfied their peasant land hunger with two hundred three and a quarter acres of swamp, cut off from civilization by a radioactive canal.

"I wonder if they're cold," Gwen said, shivering as she looked up at pine boughs sheathed in ice and topped with a frosting of snow.

"No, Gwen," George laughed. "You can't take all the poor trees inside by the fire to warm them up."

Sam and Mandy were chasing each other, discovering the fun of snow. Mandy's blackness was a vivid contrast to the white. Sam, gray going on white, blended in now and then and seemed to disappear. Mandy, the larger, threw herself on Sam and tumbled him. Sam rose, shook, examined nearby trees with a calculating eye, lifted one leg and let fly at a sapling pine.

"Old Sam's warming up one of them," George said.

"They shudder when a dog comes near," Gwen said.

"My wife, the nut."

"I talk to trees," she said, keeping her face straight.

"You didn't do too well with those African violets," George said. Hands in pockets, they were walking back toward the house.

"I didn't know about talking to them then."

"Aaaarg," he groaned. "That's the trouble with teaching women to read."

"It's not just a crazy idea," she said. "They feel. Plants feel. They appreciate it when they're watered. They faint when they're threatened with violence."

"I know a few trees that are going to have severe and fatal fainting spells," George said. "I'm going to buy a chain saw and cut some wood for the fireplace." A large deposit of snow, loosened by the heat of the sun, fell.

It splattered down from a high limb, going down his neck.

"See," Gwen said, giggling. "They heard you."

She helped gather wood when the snow was gone and the warmer weather had returned. There was a wealth of fallen trees and dead limbs for starting fires in the big fireplace, and plenty of the resin-filled longleaf pine, called fat-wood, to kindle. George bought his chain saw and felled oak. It sizzled greenly on the fire, burned for a long time, and sent out waves of heat.

With the fire, hot chocolate and cheese toast in the early evenings, and music on the four big speakers in the main room, the cozy winter passed. It was spring before it occurred to Gwen that not once had they had anyone in the house. Telephone men, meter readers, and a stray insurance salesman had knocked on the door, but not once had there been a guest in the house. George knew almost everyone in the area and kept Gwen up-to-date on gossip. She had met many of the local people while hanging around George's shop or doing the groceries in the local markets, but neither of them had expressed a desire to invite people to the house.

"Who needs people?" George asked, when Gwen talked about the situation in early March.

"I don't know," she said. "I guess I'm just a worry-wart. I keep thinking that we're too happy, too smug, too content with ourselves. Perhaps we should share it."

4

"Soft living and good food," Gwen said. George was nude, standing in front of the mirror in the bedroom and examining his waistline with a critical eye. He had saddlebags.

"You're too good to me," he said.

"We could start playing tennis," she suggested.

"Push-ups is the thing," he grinned. "With a living mat underneath me."

"My husband the sex fiend," she said.

"Rape, rape," he said, advancing on her. She squealed in mock fear and struggled, but only briefly.

"Turn off the light," she said.

"No."

She closed her eyes. It was still there, deep inside her, that old shame. But then it was buried underneath their matched passions. He laughed, however, when she threw on a robe before walking to the bathroom.

"My wife the prude," he said.

But it was better. She liked it that way. Theirs was a good, sensuous relationship. She felt so very, very close to him during the sex act, after her initial reluctance was gone. No covers these days; and after the first few moments of unease, she could bear the light. George liked to see.

She was improving with age. At twenty-seven, her thighs had gained enough muscle and weight almost to close the gap between them. Her hips had spread into a womanly beauty. Her skin was smooth, soft, and taut. Her face had thinned and her features seemed to be coming together. Her nose, once seemingly too long, was now merely a nose of great character, with delicate lines. Her mouth was her good point, along with her arched eyebrows and her brown eyes. She'd taken to wearing her hair in a sophisticated pull-back.

"For an old broad, you're pretty sharp," George would say. Then, when he gained weight during that long, cozy, happy winter, he said, "I'm going to start exercising. I'm not going to go to pot when you're getting better looking."

He came home with a big-wheeled lawn mower. Gwen smote her forehead and said, "My husband the nut. A lawnmower and no grass."

"This is no lawnmower," he said, "but a miniature brush hog."

So George mowed his trees. In the cleared area around the house, squirrels worked endlessly, teasing the dogs and the cat, digging holes, planting acorns, and forgetting them. The natural fall of acorns helped, so that with early spring the small, green oak shoots were prolific. In addition, a fern seemed to have the ability to grow overnight. While Sam and Mandy ran and barked excitedly at the spitting, buzzing lawnmower, Gwen sat on the deck and watched George mow trees. The lawnmower was a powerful one. George, once he had mowed the cleared areas, could move into the nearby brush and take down young trees up to three feet tall and almost half an inch thick. However, the mower complained at this and stray pieces of dead wood made clanking noises and nicked the blades. George attacked the brush in another fashion, with a new ax, cutting the brush below ground level so as not to have stubs sticking up. Gwen helped with the operation, stacking cut brush to burn. They had a cold beer over the fire at the end of the afternoon. The new brush, heavy with sap, burned with a crackling hiss. The fire was fed by deadwood piled at the bottom. A thorny vine, which grew with profusion, dangling and climbing into the tallest trees, burned with cracks and snaps almost as loud as small firecrackers.

In pulling down the vines, George stuck thorns into his hands. "Burn, you mothers," he said, with mock anger. "Serves you right. I hope it does hurt." He grinned at Gwen. "See that big thorny bastard over there? I'm going to cut it and burn it. Faint with fear, you bastard."

He was teasing her. She smiled.

"What I thought was, we'd gradually clear out all of the underbrush and some of the smaller trees between here and the marsh," George said.

"Yes," she agreed. "It's a shame to waste the view."

That long Saturday was filled with the snarl of the chain saw, the popping of the lawn mower, and the sharp, solid sound of the ax biting into wood. The fire was kept going, burning until darkness forced them to halt the great pioneering clearing operation. George, exhausted, came out of the shower after Gwen, mixed a tall one, and fell into a soft old chair with new gold velvet upholstery. Gwen felt good. The exercise had stimulated her. She slept well, at first, when they went to bed.

She awoke with the clammy stench of nightmare on her body, cold sweat, a deep, gnawing dread in her. The dream had been vague but powerful. Terrible pain. Legs being severed, cold metal biting in. Eyes wide, she tried to dispel the feeling. Around her, the house seemed to be alive. Still settling, expanding and contracting with the heat of the spring sun followed by a cool night, it cracked and groaned. The wind had come up during the night. The day had been unusually calm for March. Now there was a rushing hiss of gusts and an occasional clatter of screens as the gusts pounded the house. She remembered the fire. They'd left it smouldering. She got up, the cool of the night drying the perspiration from her limbs. In a pajama top, the only night garment which met with George's approval, she walked out of the bedroom into the hall.

Something cracked in front of her and her heart leaped. But it was her house, her friendly house. She pushed on, guiding herself in total darkness to the living room, and felt her way across. The outside was black, for the moon was covered by clouds. She stood in front of the glass doors and peered into the darkness. There was a glow of red at the edge of the clearing where they'd built the fire. As she watched, wind whipped sparks away. A flaming picture hit her, a visual image of the woods burning, great sheets of red leaping up and leaves steaming, cracking with the heat, and burning with sizzling bursts of fire. The vision seemed to hurt, sending sheets of pain through her.

Behind her there was a sound. She whirled and tried to see into the darkness of the living room. There was only shadow and deeper shadow, and she felt the old, familiar near-panic of night fear.

"This is my house," she told herself. She walked carefully, her eyes wide, head not turning but her eyes flicking from side to side. In the darkness, her eyes played tricks, picking up motion at the far edge of her peripheral vision. Her hand was shaking and the cold sweat of fear was back as she stabbed once, twice, three times before finding the light switch and flooding the room with blessed light.

George was hard to arouse. When he could understand, she told him the wind was blowing and the fire was in danger of spreading. He rose, groaning, went with her to the living room, turned out the light so that he could see outside, watched the glow of embers in the wind and shrugged. "It'll be all right," he said.

"Shouldn't we go out and put it out or cover it with dirt or something?"

He groaned, stretching already stiff muscles. "You go if you're so worried."

He left her, stumbling back to fall into the bed. She almost ran out of the room, fighting the need to look behind her, although her reason told her that the shadows were nothing more than her familiar furniture. She had difficulty getting back to sleep. She did not dream again, but there was pain in her legs when she awoke, the achy pain of sore muscles. That and nothing more.

George, too, was stiff. He made a great show of it and demanded tender treatment, which he received, with a special breakfast and a rub-down afterwards. Then, in spite of his new blisters on his hands, he was determined to get back to his pioneering operation. "Work the stiffness out," he said.

It was another lovely day. They began work just before noon that Sunday. They cut and hacked and mowed and sawed and chopped their way into the tangled growth, piling brush high, burning it. It was rewarding work because their progress was so visible. The area in front of the house began to take on a parklike look. They left the larger trees, which were thickly spaced, selected patterns to be left in the smaller growth, left all pines to help form a carpet of mulch with fallen pine needles, and they trimmed holly and yaupon so that they would grow more shapely. The lawnmower mulched leaves and twigs, leaving a carpet of brown behind them.

They had sandwiches on the deck overlooking the clear pond, followed them with cold beer, went back at it and hacked away a swatch of underbrush, which was burned in early evening darkness.

Gwen slept fitfully, with vague dreams. On Monday morning she was sore in every muscle.

Birds and squirrels loved the newly cleared area, scratching and digging happily. The squirrels drove the two outside dogs almost into hysterics. They were brazen little animals, coming to within a few feet of a sleeping dog, chattering, and then beating a hasty retreat when the dog aroused himself and gave chase.

By Wednesday, when George took a half-day off, Gwen was moving with more ease. George was fascinated with the clearing operation. They spent the afternoon cutting and burning, and the view was opening up. George talked about clearing all around the clear pond and then cutting bridle paths through the woods. Gwen said he certainly was ambitious. He said he'd already lost two pounds.

Gwen enjoyed the outside work. It was pleasantly warm, the sun was brilliant. There was enough wind to cool freshly created sweat, and it was sort of nice, at the end of the day, to look back and see where they had cut, the parklike, clear spaces under the trees, the openness in direct contrast to the lush growth of spring in the surrounding woods. She liked the fires, too. A cold beer was fine after hours of hard work bending, stacking, pulling, carrying, and cutting. She was the official tree shaper, armed with a small saw, powerful clippers, and a critical eye. Soft green branches fell as she shaped and patterned. Limbs too low to the ground fell to the saw.

She attributed her restless sleep to the tiredness of her body. The vague dreams were disturbing, but dreams were no new thing to her. As a child, she had always dreamed, in color, in painful vividness, and her dreams had almost always been bad. Child dreams were running in some thickness which slowed her movements to a crawl, while an unseen but terrible something closed in on her. Child dreams were being in a school room, suddenly discovering that she was naked. Her brush-clearing dreams were more vague, forgotten when she awoke save for a faint sense of unease, and were associated, she felt, with her aching muscles. This, she felt, would pass. Exercise never hurt anyone.

The change in her feelings toward the house bothered her more than the fitful sleep and the dreams. The friendly house had become just a house, a space of darkness and shadow. A childish feeling of threat.

In addition, her old hang-ups were making themselves felt. She was unable to achieve the feeling of abandonment, missed it, resorted to faking her climaxes when George wanted to make love during the day or with the lights on. She felt an overwhelming urge to drag the protective covers over her body to hide the shameful act, but fought this urge. She was not going to disappoint George, was determined not to have to hear questions, should she reveal that she was having a relapse into the neuroticism of her younger years.

Days alone in the house were filled with make-do tasks. She was becoming a perfectionist housekeeper. When George complained, she laughed at herself. "Is it that bad?"

"Honey, I can't even lay down my hat without you hanging it up in the closet, and it's been so long since I've used a dirty ashtray I feel indecently tidy. Do you know that you're gotten up three times already to empty this one particular ashtray?"

They were watching television. She had, she realized, been more interested in watching George, and leaping up to clean the ashtray after each of his cigarettes, than in watching the program.

"Find something to occupy yourself," he said. "Take a lover. Get a hobby."

"Sure," she said.

She drove the M.G. into town the next day, bought sixty dollars' worth of art supplies, moved things around in the studio room, and became an artist. George examined her efforts, kept as a surprise, and grinned. "Looks like trees," he said.

"Gee, thanks."

"Why in red?"

"Why?" She shrugged. "It's not really red. Sort of maroon. They look that way in the mornings with the sun on them."

"Send that gal to an eye doctor," George said. He

hugged her. "Go, girl. I'm pleased to see you interested in something." He laughed. "Even red trees."

She'd taken art lessons, knew the basics of composition and the handling of colors, but had, she felt, precious little talent. But she liked the fresh smell of the paints and the ting of turpentine. She spent long hours, while George was working, in the studio. Her subject was almost invariably the view out the windows, toward the marsh. Trees.

"Trees again?" George would ask.

"I'm going to become the definitive painter of twisted oaks," she said.

"When are you going to clean up this outhouse?" George asked playfully.

"You're never satisfied. When I was a perfect wife you complained. When I let the work go, being a genius seriously involved in putting every variety of tree onto canvas, you complain."

"Just as long as you don't sublimate your sex urge into your work," he teased.

The trees fascinated her, held her, dominated her. She thought trees, painted trees, dreamed trees. George cut trees, burned trees. The great American pioneer was to the creek, and spreading out, clearing around the clear pond now, being noisy and sweaty and happy, bellowing his songs as he worked, calling to Gwen to get the lead out with the cold beer.

Gwen dreamed that a furry little animal with long, sharp teeth was crawling over her body, chewing, taking her flesh, biting into her soft breasts, decapitating her nipples. She woke, screaming.

"Wha, wha," George mumbled, sitting up.

"Nothing," she said. "Just a dream."

"Honey, go to sleep," he said, wrapping her in his arms, all warm and moist and very male and dear to her. She slept in his arms and did not wake.

5

April's warmth produced a forest of bracken fern in the cleared areas. George frowned at them. They were messing up his personal park. With malice in his eyes for all intruding plants, he attacked, pushing the big-wheeled lawnmower over the clearing and wrapping it around trees to cut the small shoots which grew next to the trunks, bare-headed, a handkerchief knotted as a sweatband around his forehead, chest bare, muscles being hardened by his work.

Gwen watched from the deck. She hadn't been sleeping well. The power company people were digging a catch basin for spoil material directly across the waterway. On quiet nights the sound of earth movers and drag lines came and went with the movements of the wind. Fortunately, the work on the ocean side had been discontinued temporarily, so the drag line there, a huge thing, was quiet.

The warm sun lulled her into relaxation. The angry snarl of the lawnmower, close at hand, was a friendly noise, their own noise. It was steady. She dozed.

She heard a voice, perhaps George's voice, but deepened, made hollow as if it reverberated inside a tin tunnel. "Underneath all fear is the fear of death. Pain is bearable, if we know it is a temporary pain. We have faith in our healing ability, but when we feel some irreparable happening, that is true terror." A bulky form came at her. As in her childhood dreams, she seemed to be rooted to the ground, unable to move, swaying, making scant progress, fighting the force which held her. The mass roared down on her, huge teeth snapping at her. The mouth closed, clashing metal teeth, and she screamed once before she felt the tender flesh being punctured and rendered. Her upper body fell, ripped from her legs and stomach and hips, and blinding terror caused beads of perspiration as she sat upright with a jerk. There was a terrible pain in her chest. She called weakly, then screamed, her lungs emptying themselves in the effort. George heard her over the snarl of the mower, cut off the engine and ran to her.

"Maybe you're pregnant," he said, when she'd explained her fright. "Does it still hurt?" He was kneeling beside her, his hair damp with his sweat and his forehead band blackened and wet. "We'll run into town and see a doctor."

"No," she said, eased. "It's all right now."

However, after more nights of eerie dreams, she went to work with George and then sat in a doctor's office for most of the morning before being escorted into an examination room. She described her symptoms, the sleeplessness, the constant feeling of tiredness, and the unexplained pains which seemed to disappear when she was fully awake. She was not pregnant, although she and George were doing nothing to prevent it. Her major organs seemed to be working well. Her red cell count was a little low. She left the office after being assured that she was in basic good health and filled a prescription for vitamins and iron.

"He said I'm nuts," she told George, as he puttered, head and face hidden inside a TV set.

"For that we have to pay money?"

"No, really. He said it was probably a reaction to the change. He said that whether or not I realized it I was probably deeply affected by the death of your parents and then the move into totally new surroundings, the excitement of building a new house and all. In short, he said it was just nerves."

"What have you got to worry about?" George asked,

coming up for air and looking at her seriously. "You've got a rich, charming, handsome sex fiend for a husband, a beautiful house, two hundred three and a quarter acres of swamp cut off from the world by a radioactive canal. You're probably the best painter of twisted oak trees in the Western world. So what's the worry?"

"No worry," she said. "It's just—" There was no word for it. It was just. Just that she was a fruitcake having nightmares which freaked her out?

She shopped for groceries, spent a pleasant hour talking with a dirty old man in a fantastic little junk shop, examined new books in the library, parked the M.G. on the waterfront and watched the working fishing boats come home with huge king mackerel, dolphin, and snappers, picked up George at four-thirty. At home she threw two club steaks into the oven, fried potatoes, opened a can of small green peas, and served a good Spanish wine. After dinner, George, feeling happy, stuffed, and relaxed, opened the gin and tonic season. She drank too much too fast, danced to thunderous music with the amplifier turned up full blast, so loud that the music could probably have been heard across the marsh and waterway in Ocean City, got gloriously giddy and silly, and wrestled on the rug with George, losing, of course. She slept soundly, to wake with a sour stomach and an aching head.

George was infuriatingly cheerful. He ate four eggs and drank half a tall can of V-8 juice and kidded her about her hangover. "At least I slept well," she said.

"So the answer is to become an alcoholic," he said.

"God, the cure is worse than the ailment," she moaned, coming back to life slowly with a tall glass of ice water on top of coffee and V-8 juice.

That was the day Mandy died.

Feeling yucky and slightly suicidal, the usual after too much booze, she put on her private sun-bathing bikini and lounged on the balcony over the clear pond, letting the sun help, her sweat out the booze.

The dogs drank from the clear pond. This had worried Gwen at first, but George had sampled the water himself and declared it "fittin'." He'd even sent a sample off to the state lab to have it analyzed. It showed a few harmless bacteria and some phosphates, which explained the clear green color, but it was pronounced harmless to livestock. So the dogs drank there and played there. Mandy, part hound with, perhaps, a bit of Labrador, loved the water and went into it often with great, bounding splashes. She was a loving dog, always full of spirit. So when Gwen noticed her staggering toward the clear pond, her attention was engaged immediately.

The big, black dog drank endlessly, and then staggered, feet crossing, to vomit into the sand. Gwen called her. The dog lifted her head but fell weakly. Gwen hurried to her. The dog's eyes were large, the pupils dilated. As Gwen neared, she saw the dog squat to urinate and then stagger back to drink from the pond.

Gwen half-carried the animal to the balcony, where she petted her, talked to her, and offered sympathy. When the dog's rapid breathing slowed early in the afternoon, Gwen thought she was recovering, but the breathing lessened until, just before Gwen ran in to dress, it was painfully infrequent and the dog seemed almost comatose.

Gwen strained to lift the dog into the back of the pickup truck, drove hurriedly into town, and stopped by the repair shop to tell George that Mandy was terribly sick. Mandy died on the way to the nearby small city, convulsing and then going into a coma from which she did not recover.

"Do you have any neighbors who don't like dogs?" the veterinary asked.

"No neighbors at all," Gwen said, having dried her tears.

"I hesitate to suggest it," the veterinary said, "but the way you describe her symptoms makes it sound like poison. Do you put out rat poison or anything?"

She shook her head.

"All I can do, Mrs. Ferrier, is perform an autopsy," he shrugged. "If you care to go to that expense."

"Yes," she said. "I'd like to know, at least." She was searching her mind, feeling vague guilt. Had she or George left out some poison? She could think of none. She drove home slowly, saddened. A brief letter arrived from the animal hospital three days later. Mandy, said the report, had apparently eaten of *Datura stramonium*, known as jimson-weed or Thornapple. The autopsy had found considerable amounts of hyoscyamine, atropine, scopolamine, and hyoscine, alkaloids common to the nightshade family of plants. It was, the vet reported with obvious pride, a rare case. It would probably be written up in a veterinary journal, since dogs seldom ate the poisonous weed, the few reported cases of jimson-weed poisoning in the state having been confined, in the past, to cattle and sheep.

"I'll be damned," George said. "We're harboring killers on our estate." He was touched by Gwen's sadness, but, man-like, he would not admit his own feeling of loss over a mere dog. "I'll take my trusty mower and lop off the heads of all the jimson-weed killers I can find."

Gwen spoke quickly, without thinking. "They were only trying to—"

"To what?" George asked, looking at her questioningly.

"—to warn us," she finished, with a weak little shrug and a smile.

"They who?"

"Oh, forget it," she said. It was so silly. She could not understand why she had said such a foolish thing.

For days Gwen kept Sam, the surviving outside dog, in

the house. He was fretful and restless, wanting to be outside to chase squirrels and enjoy the spring sun. She forgot to call him back from a morning outing and he once again roamed the woods, barking at the elusive tree dwellers and looking for Mandy.

Satan, the black ex-tom, was also an outdoor animal in warm weather. He showed off by climbing trees. He stalked birds with murderous intent but, fortunately for the birds, hunted with a casualness bred of good food and lazy living.

Meanwhile, Pine Tree Island's own Paul Bunyan felled a forest of small brush. He worked in the evenings, becoming hard and muscular with the exercise, and cleared more and more as he moved around the house toward the clear pond. He planned his clearing as a general would plan a battle, walking ahead of his operation to consider the situation and the terrain before axing his way slowly through the brush.

"It's the instinct of an Indian fighter," he said. "In the old days on the frontier, they cut down all the trees around the house so that Injuns couldn't sneak up from tree to tree to do them in. When I'm finished, we'll be safe from bill collectors and magazine salesmen. Nary a one of them can sneak up on us."

Gwen checked out books from the library. She remembered happy Mandy and was curious about the poisonous plant which she'd eaten. With the aid of books, she identified jimson-weed, growing on the far side of the clear pond. In addition, she identified a half dozen other varieties of more or less poisonous plants. Poison oak, ivy, and sumac were there in abundance. There was also some white snakeroot; hundreds of bracken fern, a cumulatively poison plant when eaten by animals; polkweed, a poisonous plant whose leaves were often eaten by people after proper cooking as a green; fumewort; and rattleweed.

And, to compound her astonishment at the variety of plants which could kill or weaken, she discovered that the common oak, the most plentiful tree on the island, could poison with large amounts of tannic acid and a volatile oil if animals ate young shoots and leaves in quantity. Pines were poison. Some lilies were poison. Tobacco plants, if eaten by cattle, were poison. Dozens of varieties of plants caused effects ranging from itching and breaking out to painful death.

She shared her knowledge with George, who treated it lightly. "Murderer," he said, kicking at an oak tree.

The mower roared, the ax flew, and the chain saw snarled. There was a pile of neatly stacked fireplace wood large enough to last for years. And the house was beginning to stand out from the woodlands, although the happy pioneer had left plenty of trees for cover and shade in his cleared areas. He was working his way around the clear pond, working also into late May, when the days had begun to show the promise of summer. He would end his work with a nude swim in the pond, and come up puffing and dripping to have his drink and dinner on the balcony, insisting on the outdoor bit in spite of vicious deer flies and mosquitoes. And his mornings began, as he'd dreamed, with a plunge into chill, clear water. His body, trimmed by the hard work, would slice into the water and disappear into the cool depths. He'd panic Gwen by staying under for impossible lengths of time, surfacing halfway across the pond.

Gwen began to live in shorts and bathing suits, but she was not, as yet, attracted to the water. "I need an outside temperature of at least ninety and a water temperature approximating a warm bath," she would tell George when he coaxed her to join him in his twice daily swims.

She was sleeping slightly better, but her nights were still troubled by dreams. The dreams seemed to follow a pattern having to do with dismemberment and death. "You sonofabitch," she told George, while discussing a dream with him, a particularly violent dream in which she had felt the pain of having both arms severed from her body, "you planted it in my mind with your talk about fears. Before that I was content with being chased by unseen monsters and being unable to move."

"Your problem, kid, is that you need a—"

"—a good screw," she finished for him.

On a Wednesday in early June, she got a good screw. If the treatment had been applied lovingly by Dr. George, the foremost practitioner of anti-lackanookie medicine, it would not have been unusual. However, this particular treatment was applied by a surprised and delighted meter reader from the rural electric cooperative. The effect on Gwen was much more than surprise.

6

At first she thought she was going mad and bounced words such as "schizophrenia" around in her muddled mind. Certainly, the girl who had performed that animal act on the chaise longue on the balcony, in broad daylight, was not Gwen Ferrier.

"Ummm," that girl had said, spread-eagled, filled with relaxing man, "there'll be more of *that.*"

That girl declined the half-embarrassed offer of a handkerchief. "I have this," that girl said, pulling on her bikini bottom with sensual motions, displaying her body with pride even after the act. "*This*" was soaked with semen, a stained, horrible object held in a trembling hand, held at a distance, the offensive, musky odor of semen wafting upward to cause nausea in Gwen's now hot, now cold body.

"I'd like for there to be more," the meter reader had said.

"Call first," that girl had said, actually reaching down to seize the limp member which, moments before, had been the point of concentration for her entire being.

That girl had still been in command when the meter reader walked jauntily away and rounded a corner. That girl was no longer present when the sound of the meter reader's pick-up truck faded down the road. Instead, it was Gwen, holding her bikini top in front of still-moist breasts, breasts which reeked with the tobacco and male odor of the meter reader's mouth. Gwen, back from a far place, screamed, exposing her breasts as she clamped one hand, filled with bikini top, to her mouth, and bit into a finger with painful force. It was Gwen, sobbing hysterically, who ran into the bath, vomited, ripped off the bikini bottom, and stared, horror-stricken, at the tell-tale moistness there. It was Gwen, face tear-stained and drawn, who sat on the red and gold sofa in the living room, George's bird-shooting shotgun, loaded, near her lips. She was nude. The inner portions of her thighs were sticky. She felt calm, sure of her decision. Her right toe could reach the trigger. The double-barreled muzzle of the shotgun stretched her lips as she opened her mouth.

Now.

There was no note. She could not bear to think of telling him. He would find her. She'd be nude and soiled with the seed of another man. The autopsy would show it. Then he'd know without her having to verbalize it or write it down. He'd know.

George. George.

The basic fear is that of death.

"Once," he'd said, "you had another fear, the fear of having your chastity taken by force. Since that is no longer possible, your fear must be the basic fear of death."

But he was wrong. She welcomed death. It crooked a bony finger at her and grinned in welcome. It was cold, blued steel in her mouth, the sharp, hard edges of the trigger on her toe. For she had ruined her life. In all her life she'd never had anyone to love her for herself, had never had anyone to love. Then George had come and it had been incredibly beautiful. Her love for George and his for her had conquered. Together, they'd made her almost human, had killed the darkness in her. No. It hadn't been killed. It had merely retreated, to creep up on her in a different guise.

"Sorry," the meter reader had said, halting in mid-stride as he came around the house and, his head level with the balcony, looked up to see a woman in a bikini lying face down on the chaise longue. She had loosened the tie-top. Her breasts were resting on the small scrap of cloth, but the bulging sides were exposed to the sun and to his view. She'd pushed the tiny bottom down until it was a mere string crossing under her buttocks.

"I didn't know anyone was here," the meter reader said, backing off.

"Just me," the girl said, sitting up, holding the halter loosely in front of her breasts, and smiling.

What had happened then was so incredible that it halted her, froze her hand on the shotgun, her mind remembering and being astounded. She had always tried to know herself. She had taken several psychology courses in her search for herself. Now she found that her curiosity was not dead. Death, waiting, folded his arms patiently. He had the rest of the afternoon. Meanwhile, she questioned the afternoon's events. Why had they happened?

She had been at one with the world. She was a living entity merged into the whole. She dozed in the sun, her skin oiled. She felt lazy and comfortable. She felt as if she could sleep forever and not dream, and yet she was not asleep. She could hear the wind in the treetops and the far rumble of the heavy equipment. They were digging the canal on the inland side of the waterway. Work continued on the spoil basin as machines pushed up dikes fifteen feet high to hold the mud and living shells and broken grass which would, when the dredges began work, be pumped back across the waterway into the basin. There it would stand, a two-mile-long, fifteen-foot-high mesa of stinking, reeking mud, smelling of ages of rotting vegetation, dead oysters, and salt marsh. But the equipment sounds were distant and familiar. Those sounds acted as a soporific, lulling her into the most delicious state of drowsiness she'd known in weeks. And into that pleasant state came thoughts, feelings, and an awareness which, in retrospect, was druglike. She was on some kind of high. Like most young people, she'd experimented with drugs of the milder variety, grass, once a good grade of hash. And yet the high was not the dulled, stuporous, out-of-it thing which came with drugs. It was a clearheaded realization that she was breathing, living. She felt the flood of blood in her body, and felt the function of her organs. Strange things happened to her ears, without seeming at the time to be strange. She could hear, the sound of the wind and heavy equipment only a background, the warm hum of a bee; she could feel the moisture of the earth, the sweetness of it, the delicate giving of soft particles under bare feet as she walked through newly plowed Illinois loam. She was more aware of the sun; and she could feel its life-giving rays entering her, penetrating warm. There was a sense of timelessness in her awareness. Thoughts moved with pleasing slowness, crawling, possessing her. Every nerve ending was alive, and individual cells pleasured themselves as a hot, spreading sexual awareness crept up and over from her nether regions and engulfed her.

There, just beyond her reach, was the answer. Some

magic of mind, some lunacy of brain, had moved her outside of herself, leaving the frailties of Gwen Ferrier behind, and forcing away her natural and induced inhibitions. She stretched languidly, knowing her body as she'd never known it before, ignoring a small, clamorous voice deep inside which questioned, screamed negation of her newness.

He came floating into her awareness as a spore slowly floats on the wind. Fertile, natural, ripe, she sat up, holding the halter in front of her tingling breasts. "Come here," she said, letting the halter fall. It seemed to take forever for the gaily colored piece of cloth to fall and drape itself over her bare leg.

"Look, lady," the man said, looking around nervously.

"Don't talk," she said, holding out her arms, her breasts aching with ripeness. A bee buzzed and settled into the open petals of a wildflower beside the clear pond. She sensed it, knew it, felt the penetration of its honey-gathering tube, and knew the ripe feeling of merged pollen. She held her arms out, smiling. No question of morality. No right. No wrong. It was the way things were. Fertile, ripe, passive, she accepted him, eased his fevered haste, and bathed him in the sweet juices of her body. Abandoned, wild, silent.

The thing which hurt most was her inability to remember a single time when she'd been so at peace with George. Never, in seven years of marriage to a passionate man, had she known the quiet-thick, pleasure-ripeness of it. Never had she so opened herself, willingly, peacefully, exquisitely ecstatic. Never had her inner tissue drunk so thirstily of male juices.

That she was pregnant was unquestionable. That and that alone could explain the beauty of it.

To release the safety, she had to invert the gun. The

small metal button moved with a click. The weapon took on new meaning. Now it was ready to play its role. Deadly, small things inside its blue metal tubing were tense, ready to leap forward, and perform their function.

She was calm. There was no answer. She could live a dozen lifetimes and not know why she'd done it.

She positioned the weapon slowly and carefully. She kissed the cold metal with parted lips, an obscene kiss while death grinned and waited. Her mouth was open, teeth grating on metal. She positioned her foot and wiggled her toe experimentally. She had, according to George, toes like a monkey, movable, small, and thin.

"Please understand," she thought.

Only an outward push on her right leg held her from death and relief from the unbearable guilt. She tensed, took one last, long, slow breath, and held it. The explosion was not gunpowder and shot but a living thing, a big, long-clawed black housecat named Satan, leaping from the floor, all claws extended, throwing his lithe body through the air to knock the weapon from her hands. It fell, hit the cushions, and slid to the thick carpet with a thud. No explosion. Startled, she looked at a familiar creature changed into a raging beast. The cat had landed on the sofa and regarded her balefully, eyes cold fire, fangs exposed, a rumble coming from its throat.

"Satan?"

Animals feel things. She knew that. It was incredible. He was trying to save her life. "You're wrong, old fellow," she said, quite calmly, reaching for the gun. Long marks sprang up on her bare arm. The cat's movement had been so swift that she saw only the results, blood welling up from deep scratches. She gasped. "Satan?"

There was something familiar about the way the cat was acting. It came to her. Hot August sun. Dusty vegetation drying in the sun. Pushing through uncleared woods and brush to face an opossum. There was the same strange feeling of threat.

The cat stood between her and what she must do. She aimed a light blow at him and missed. She was rewarded by scratches on the back of her hand, delivered with lightning quickness as the hand flashed past. Knowing a new kind of fright, she rose. The cat stalked, its back arched, to the end of the sofa. It pounced, leaving a bloody trail of claw marks down her naked thigh before landing on its feet and advancing toward her, making that horrible growling sound in its throat.

She ran. Bare breasts bobbled. She bumped the doorjamb painfully and gained the bedroom with the cat behind her, its claws digging into her calves. She screamed, leaped for the bathroom, and closed the door, narrowly missing catching the cat in it.

She did not realize, until she heard George's voice calling her, that she'd been cheated of death. Shaking with it, weak, she had spent a timeless period locked in the bathroom, hearing the scratches on the door and the rumble of the cat's growl. Then his voice.

"No," she screamed. "No, George!" The cat. The cat.

"Honey?" He was so dear to her, so beautiful. He stood there, his white coveralls mussed and soiled, looking at her as she cowered against the far wall.

"My God, Gwen." He had seen the blood, the crusted scratches. "What happened?"

"Satan," she said.

"Satan?" He could not understand. "He's asleep on the bed."

"Satan, he—"

George caught her as she fell.

7

If one is healthy, she found, one survives. The right arm, severed by a sharp blade just below the shoulder, bone crushed, jagged, can be closed off with fire. The system goes into protective shock, being unable, while aware, to bear the pain. But one survives. Loss of blood is limited by the cauterizing. There is an endless period of pain. Two arms severed at once is more of a shock to the system and can kill. Healthy specimens can, at times, survive. Life lingers on, in any case, fighting, not taking the easy way of quick death. A jagged, dull blade can dismember the body limb by limb and leave occasional periods of consciousness during which pain is a roaring rush which takes possession of all the senses. A foot lopped off bleeds the vital substances of the body into the earth. A leg chopped off causes the body to fall down, to lie on the warm earth writhing in pain.

She knew all. They took her fingers, one by one, giving her time in between to regain consciousness. Then they cut off her hands at the wrists. Then, whack, the arms at the elbow. Thunk. At the shoulders. She screamed in pain, roared with it, bellowed it, wept with it, begged them to stop, and sought death. Whisk. A foot gone. Thunk. A leg at the knee.

She was a twisting, bucking, limbless torso, flopping on bloody earth, screaming. And relief came only after an eternity of suffering. Her blood refused to run; it just oozed slowly out, taking her life with it by degrees, leaving her a dulling awareness of death and a fading pain which, she knew, was terminal. There was only a spark of life in her. Her skin was rotting, sloughing off. Inside, the bones had begun to decay, yet still there was life, agonized, dying so slowly, so slowly.

"Please, please, please."

"Gwen. Hey, Gwen. You're fine. You're all right."

She didn't even hurt.

"The doc gave you a sedative."

"George?" Tears came. "Oh, George."

"Easy, kid. You're all right. I don't know what got into that cat." His face was so concerned. "He's at the vet's. They'll have to keep him under observation. If he's rabid—" He paused grimly.

The hospital was old and small and crowded. There were no private rooms. The woman in the other bed in Gwen's room was a perky senior citizen with a new scar to indicate the removal of a non-malignant growth from her stomach. She was ambulatory and had quite an active tongue. She never slept. There was no opportunity for Gwen to talk. She had to tell a highly censored version of the event. Dr. Peter Braws, who had examined her in his office, was quite interested. He was a nice fellow, married to his office nurse, but with an eye which still appreciated femininity. Gwen told him and George that she'd been sun bathing, had come into the house to shower off the sun oil, and had been attacked without warning by the usually gentle pussycat. She felt guilty about slandering Satan. She knew why he had attacked, but with an audience she couldn't explain it. She wasn't even sure she could explain it to George.

During the first night she was under heavy sedation. It was into the next afternoon before Dr. Braws allowed her to come out of the drug haze long enough to think clearly. Then the full meaning of what had happened hit her anew and she wished, once again, for death. She could not bear to look into George's cheerful face and think of what she'd done to him and to their love. To die was still the logical answer.

George guided her tenderly to the car, after two nights in the hospital. "I just don't understand, honey," he said, as he started the car. "Braws said you were highly wrought up, and that's the question. What is it?" He didn't tell her that the doctor had said Gwen was near the point of a complete breakdown. "Is it something I've done?"

His sincerity was a knife in her heart. "Oh, no," she said. "No, no, no."

"Well, you're not to worry. I'm going to take good care of you."

He did. At home, Sam, lonely with both Mandy and Satan gone, met them with happy barks and jumps and frantic, energetic runs around and around them as they went toward the house. Inside, George led her to bed and tucked her in. He set the timer on the clock radio for her pill time. She was on a rather powerful tranquilizer which made it easy to sleep and sleep. She lost track of time. The windows were open to the spring air and it was balmy and lovely. The tranquilizers allowed her to think, but killed the pain of thinking.

"Why was the shotgun in the living room, honey?" George asked. Had it been a day, two days? She didn't answer. There was no simple answer. "You worry me, Gwen. Do you know that?"

"Yes."

"Honey, we've got it made. We've got what most people struggle for all their lives, security, most anything we want, happiness. I haven't taken a mistress or anything and I don't beat you."

There was no way of telling him.

"If anything ever happened to you, I think I'd walk into the pond and forget to come out," George said.

It wasn't fair. She was being asked to live with what

she'd become. She was no better than her mother. She'd given her body gladly and wantonly. What she had always hated and condemned, she'd become. And he was telling her she had to accept it, and live with it. By forcing her to see how badly he'd be hurt, he was making it impossible for her to seek the easy way out.

She was dozing. It was another of those glorious May afternoons. She woke with a feeling of violation and found that George had joined her on her bed. He was dressed only in a bathing suit and his hands were on her. His hands pressed, through the thin pajama top, on her breasts, where the man, whose name she didn't even know, had fondled her. "Don't," she said, without thinking.

He respected her wishes. But he was a sensuous man and he had no idea of her state of mind. That night he persisted. It was George, she told herself. Her husband. But when his hand went down to cover her feminine dampness, to press and explore, she could not hold back a near scream. She jerked away, trying not to sob aloud.

"Is that it?" George asked, not angry, just concerned. "Is it the same old gig?"

Why couldn't she just die? He lay beside her, not touching her. "Gwen?"

"You could find someone else," she said. "You're young."

"Gwen, that's crazy talk." His voice was strained. "Dr. Braws thinks, well, maybe—" She did not help him. "Well, Gwen, it would be no disgrace. I mean, lots of people need help."

She seized upon the suggestion, not because she wanted to talk to anyone, but because it would at least give her some more time to think. George drove her to the psychiatrist's office the next day. The road from Ocean City to the upriver city passed through natural woodland. Dogwoods bloomed in white splendor. The world was renewing itself in pastel green and bright colors.

It was obvious that either George or Dr. Braws or perhaps both had talked to the psychiatrist in advance. He was a kindly, bald, corpulent old man with a chubby, friendly face. She could not see herself telling this nice man that she had committed casual adultery. She said banal things about being tense without knowing the reason, about the shock of the incident with the cat. He let her talk without really saying anything for a long time. When she fell silent, he shocked her.

"Did you have the shotgun out to shoot the cat?" he asked.

"No," she said automatically. "Yes, perhaps. Oh, I don't know."

"Have you ever killed anything, Gwen?" he asked.

"No. Oh, insects. Plants."

He was silent, his head nodding. Finally, to break the silence, he asked, "Plants?"

"Isn't that silly?"

"Not at all. There's been some very interesting work done in the field. There are those who think plants have feelings, that they, for example, scream when they're plucked or broken." He was looking at her closely. "You've always been good with animals?"

"Always. They seem to like me."

"Why, do you suppose?"

"Oh, I don't know. I think they can feel the love."

"And you've never been attacked by an animal before?"

"No. Yes. Once there was an opossum." She told him. Anything to keep away from the subject of that rutting on the balcony. She was not ready to face that herself, much less share the knowledge with another.

The interview seemed aimless and meaningless. She talked when she was primed with a question. She knew she was defeating the purpose and felt guilty for wasting money just to have a friendly chat with the doctor. She knew, too, that George must have mentioned the way she felt about sex, but the doctor made no attempts to open that can of worms. He merely smiled and nodded and talked about animals, and children and plants. He was quite good, for, before the end of the hour, she was at ease with him. Feeling that she had been manipulated, she was moodily silent on the way home.

By a supreme effort of will power, she was able to perform her connubial duty with George, faking her response all the way and feeling violently nauseous. During her next interview with the psychiatrist, she brought up the subject of her dreams.

"Interesting," he said. "Why, do you suppose, are you having recurrent dreams of such a bloody nature?" She shook her head. "Have you ever seen anyone lose a limb, say in an automobile accident?"

"No."

"Have you read accounts of torture and dismemberment?"

"Oh, not really. I avoid such things usually. I guess I must have read about the Inquisition when I was in school. I can remember a few things about it, and witchcraft, I mean the methods used against so-called witchcraft. They were pretty bloody, but it has no real fascination for me. I mean, if I were touring a castle or something I wouldn't ask to be shown the dungeon and the rack and things like that."

The doctor took a surprising tack. "I understand that in some of the more primitive Arabian countries they still lop off a hand in punishment for petty theft." He studied her closely and saw a slight frown. "And the American Indians were rather inventive. There was one particular case. A novel was written about it. A Kentucky frontier woman was kidnapped by Indians. She watched them kill all of her children except for one babe in arms. Later, she witnessed that child being killed by having its head dashed out against a rock. And she was forced to watch the torture of a young white man. He was hoisted up by thongs strung through his shoulder muscles, and roasted by fire all the while. When he tried to lift his feet out of the fire, he'd put weight on his mutilated shoulder muscles. Then they cut off his limbs, cauterizing the stumps, one at a time, being careful to keep him alive as long as possible." He was looking at her through half-closed eyes. He saw her tongue flick out to lick her lips, and saw her eyes narrow in thought.

"That doesn't shock you?"

"You're going to think I'm crazy," she said evenly, "but when you've *felt* it happen to you, it loses its shock value."

"In your dreams, you mean."

"Yes, but it's so very, very real."

"Why, do you suppose?"

She smiled. "If I knew, would I be here?"

"In these dreams, are there particular people involved?"

She thought. "No. *They* are unseen. They are huge. They come at me and I'm unable to run."

"They? Men? People?"

"Yes and no. Things. Huge teeth. Metal teeth sometimes."

King grunted. He was eighty-two years old. A Freudian by training, he'd developed some rather independent ideas in thirty-five years of practice in an area of the country where psychiatry was not fully understood. He was recognized as an authority, was often used as an expert witness in court cases, and was consulted by physicians all over the Southeast. There was something about the girl which appealed to him, something which roused his interest. However, his eighty-two-year-old mind, although still sharper than many a third his age, had its moments of forgetfulness. There was something, but he couldn't place it. He had done his best, during that first visit, merely to gain a measure of ease with the patient. It was expected that the patient would withhold information and skirt as far as possible the underlying cause of the problem. In past years he had been recognized in his circle as one of the more patient men, willing to ease up on problems. But now that he was eighty-two, feeling time running out, each new case seemed to take on a sense of urgency. Dr. King didn't like unfinished things. Ideally, at some future date about which he did not care to speculate, he would close his last case, wrap it up neatly, complete his report and file it and then go to sleep in his office chair and not wake up.

"You are much too pretty to be eaten by nightmare things," he said, rising with effort, grunting, and stretching his old legs. "Please do me a personal favor and stay uneaten until you can see me next week." He smiled toward the door, indicating that she was to go. "Sooner if you like," he added.

George was in the waiting room. There were no other patients. He grinned and put both his hands on Gwen's head. "Looks as large as ever," he said.

Dr. King was in the doorway. "You have a seat, child," he said to Gwen, "while I talk with your husband. We're going to ask him to reveal all your weaknesses." He chuckled happily. "Actually," the old man said, when George had closed the office door behind him, "I just want to ask one or two questions. For example, what does she do?"

"Like when I'm working or something?" George asked.

"Like when she's alone," the doctor said. "When she has time on her hands."

"Well, she paints a little."

"Interesting. Is she involved with the painting?"

"Yes and no," George said, thinking about it. "She's not very passionate about it, I guess."

"Get her other things to do." He stifled a tired yawn. It was past his nap time. "How about children? Nothing better than a child for keeping a woman busy."

"There's nothing wrong with either of us," George said, "at least not that the docs have found. We've done nothing to keep from having a child for months now."

"She likes animals," King said. "Get her a new puppy, a very young, sickly puppy. Nag her a bit about housework, in a nice way of course. From what I can gather you two live a lonely life. Get some people around you. Work her hard. Get her interested in as many things as possible. It is too early, of course, for me to offer an opinion, but in childless women of her age, there is often a tendency to grow lazy, morbid, moody. They feel life is passing them by. They need things to do."

"O.K.," George said.

"How's your sex life?" the doctor asked bluntly.

"She didn't mention it?" George frowned in puzzlement.

"Ah," King said. "We have hit on it?"

"I'm surprised she didn't talk about it. She had some rather bad childhood experiences with her mother."

"I don't want to hear it from you," King said curtly. "From her. When she's ready."

"I think she was considering suicide," George said.

"Why, do you suppose?"

"I have no idea. Honestly, I don't. Things are touchy with the sex bit, but I don't push it."

"This is new?"

"Yes and no. It took a long time, but after a while she seemed to like it, sex. Now it's back, all the old hang-ups."

"Be strong," King said with a smile. "Don't push her. Could you, by any chance, take a few days off? Take her on a trip?"

"Yes," he said, although his shop was filled with jobs.

They took a nice little twin engine jet from the Port City, were hung up in a holding pattern waiting to get into LaGuardia, flew with the fantastic Manhattan skyline in their window for long, lovely minutes. Darkness came, and the lights sparkled up to enchant Gwen into a state of dazed appreciation. They moved at a hard pace for three days, walking the halls of museums until their legs ached, experimenting with different foods, and peeking into dark little shops, buying George a new trenchcoat at Lord and Taylor's, Gwen new things along Fifth Avenue. The second night in New York was a nice one. After wine, Italian food, and brandy, they fell into bed. They were stuffed, tired, and full of talk about the eventful day. Gwen made the advances and, in darkness, she was warm, playful, and responsive. George slept peacefully. Gwen slept so soundly that they got a late start the next day, for George would not wake her. He sat in the chair beside the bed studying her peaceful face. She was smiling. No nightmares.

She was the old Gwen, even after they drove home, late at night, with Sam crowded into the M.G. with them. He was a paroled prisoner from the animal hospital, where he'd spent the time being wormed, shot, bathed, flea-proofed, and clipped.

George remembered Dr. King's advice. He bought the runt of a Boston litter, a pup so small that it could rest comfortably on his hand. Gwen's motherly instincts were aroused. George protested playfully, on a cool late May morning, when Gwen served breakfast with the puppy tucked down inside her playsuit bra for warmth and closeness. "That's my personal territory," he growled, tweaking the puppy's ear.

"Don't be selfish," Gwen said. "There's plenty of me for both of you."

"Slut," he said.

"Why did you say that?" She had stopped in mid-movement and was looking at him tensely.

"Honey, I was teasing. That's all." He jumped up. He kissed her. "It's just that I'm infernally jealous." He growled and chewed on her ears playfully. She giggled and pushed him away, but she took the puppy out of the bra and put it in its basket near the table.

Once, in Winston-Salem, Gwen had gotten the African violet bug. In accordance with Dr. King's advice, George brought home a dozen of the lush plants from the local florist. He supplied her with all the needs for African violet culture, foods and sprays and rich potting soil. "I thought the place needed a bit of greenery," he explained.

Dr. Peter Braws and his wife were their first guests. Gwen did steaks and it was a nice evening. Then George invited two of the Ocean City fishermen and their wives, and the talk was salty and seemed to interest Gwen. She'd just returned from her second visit with Dr. King. She had gone alone, since George's work was stacked up. In the bustle of preparing dinner they had little chance to talk. "I think he's trying to determine whether or not I hated my mother and father," Gwen said, with a shrug, when George asked her about the visit.

It is often possible to hide, even from one's self, a deep and disturbing hurt. So it was with Gwen. The Boston puppy, as yet unnamed, was not eating well, had to be coaxed to drink milk from an eye dropper. Gwen was busy in a flurry of spring house cleaning. In jeans and sweatshirt, she tackled the windows inside and out, vacuumed down a few spider webs which had collected in the high corners, scrubbed fingerprints from the walls near light switches, and cleaned the carpet with a sudsy spray can and a machine rented from the Ocean City Building Supply Company. She scoured the tile of the bathrooms with Lysol, getting all traces of mildew from the joints. George, pleased with her apparent sense of well-being, worked long hours and had no time for the great American clearing operation. The African violets thrived.

"You're talking to them," George said, as Gwen muttered kind words one morning, feeding the plants which were lined up in the kitchen windows.

"Don't knock it," she said. "It works. See?"

Two of the plants were blooming. They looked healthier than when George had brought them home.

"Way to go, fella," Gwen said playfully, touching one of the flowering plants with a fingertip. "You are valiant and quite beautiful."

"Lady," George said, "when those things start turning you on, out they go."

8

June is the greenest month. By June, growing things have usually done their annual bit, pines shooting up, young pines, green, fresh, thick, a full foot. The annual weeds have come back, and woodlands which seem open in winter become clogged with verdant undergrowth. On George and Gwen's two hundred and three and a quarter acres, gentle rains and warm sun had created a junglelike denseness. After long neglect, the cleared areas were greened by bracken, young oak seedlings, tufts of tough grass, and sprouting yaupons. Small trees cut below the ground had put out new shoots. However, it was all tender, young growth and fell easily to the whirling blades of the powerful mower.

After the hot job, George swam in the clear pond. He had picked up a face mask and a pair of flippers. He would dive for what seemed to Gwen to be an endless period, and then surface, puffing and blowing, calling out to her that she should see. It was hot, in the high eighties. There was no breeze. Gwen allowed herself to be coaxed into the water, wading out gingerly. The edge of the pond was covered by tall, straight grass which grew a few inches into the shallow water. There, the grass was replaced by a soft, pulpy growth which seemed to cover the bottom and, underfoot, was slick.

"Yuk," Gwen said, stepping gingerly. She fell forward, swam with an awkward crawl stroke. She was not a water baby. George dived, came up under her, and pinched her on the rump. She squealed and turned toward the shore, gained shallow water, and made faces as she waded through the slimy vegetation. "It feels as if you might step on a snake at any moment," she said.

"I think that's one reason why the pond is so clear," George said, his face mask pushed up on his forehead. "The bottom is covered with it. Out in the deep parts it grows three feet high."

"Yeech," Gwen said.

"But the water is warm, isn't it?" George said.

"Warm enough."

"Cheaper than a swimming pool, too."

"You can have it. It feels like worms."

"Tell you what, I'll clear a little beach for you. Cut out the grass so we'll have just nice, white sand, and then cut the stuff off the bottom out for a ways."

"I sort of like it the way it is," Gwen said.

"But not to swim in."

"You can swim enough for me."

"Party pooper," he said, splashing her.

While George swam and dived, she picked her way gingerly around the margin of the pond. At the low end, near the low, damp, marshy area, she made a discovery. She squatted, making a pleased sound. The plant which had attracted her attention was unlike anything she'd ever seen. Several pulpy, pale green stems supported bright red, teeth-lined maws. "George," she called.

He swam slowly toward her.

An ant was crawling on the plant. It stopped and

started, climbed a stem, seemed excited, dashed into the red area. It crawled over a tiny, black, hairlike protrusion in the field of red. In the blink of an eye, the plant moved, jaws closing, enfolding the ant inside.

"Yeah," George said, kneeling beside her. "Venus-flytrap. How about that?"

"It just ate an ant," Gwen said wonderingly.

"The law of survival," George said.

There was a colony of them in the low, boggy area. Dozens. Each had multiple traps. George caught ants and dropped them into the traps. When the ant struck one of the trigger hairs, the trap snapped shut in about a half second.

"It's the oddest thing I've ever seen," Gwen said. Reading about it, she discovered that she was not the first to be impressed by the Venus-flytrap. It had been amazing botanists since its discovery in 1760. Charles Darwin called it the "most wonderful" plant in the world. An old *National Geographic* article, dug out of the library's collection, explained how to keep the plant indoors. Gwen, having spent portions of several days observing the plants, decided to risk moving a few. She carefully dug out coned earth sections, the flytraps atop, and transplanted them into a large planter filled with the acid, boggy soil. The plants thrived. George captured house flies and fed the plants. An active fly could escape before the trap closed. George pulled off wings to slow the insects.

"Ugg," Gwen said, the first time he did it. "You're *that* sort of lad."

"Better I should poison them with fly spray or squash them with a swatter?" George watched a trap close on a struggling fly. "Buddhist," he said idly. "They're *your* flesh-eating monsters."

"Wouldn't it be great," he said later, "if they grew to tremendous size? Make a great science fiction movie. Huge, man-eating plants. A scantily clad beauty being engulfed in the closing red maw. Tarzan to the rescue, fighting with his muscles bulging to rescue the gal."

Gwen fed ants to the flytraps.

"Poor ants," George teased, remembering how she'd shuddered at his pulling the wings off flies.

"Poor plants," Gwen said, with seriousness. "The soil is poor, not at all suited to them. They have to have the basic protein from the insects to supplement what they can get from the poor soil. Where they came from they didn't need to be carnivorous."

"What?" George said, looking at her.

"What what?" she asked, musing over the plants.

"You said where they came from they didn't need to be carnivorous. Way I heard it, they're native to a small area of the North Carolina coast."

"Oh, yes," she said, still bemused. "Did I say that?"

"You did."

"Hummm. Just the idlings of an idle mind, I guess."

George went in for a shower. She looked into space. Why had she said that, about where they came from? For a moment, at the time she had been speaking, she had known. Now it was not clear. It rather frightened her, for she had been, in that instant, a different person. In retrospect, the feeling made her even more uneasy, for once before she'd been someone else. "*Come here.*" She could hear the words in her mind and see the doubtful, hopeful look on the meter reader's face.

"Is it normal," she asked Dr. King during her next session, "to feel, at times, as if you're someone else?"

"Why do you ask?"

She shrugged. She'd had the dream again, for the first time in weeks. It had been an especially painful dream involving dismemberment. She felt as if she'd betrayed both George and herself.

"I don't know, really," she said. "The other day I said something, that's all. Something which I wouldn't ordinarily say."

"Tell me about it."

"I was watching the Venus-flytraps," she began. "I said," she paused. She tried to form the words. Suddenly her mind went blank. She shook her head as if dazed.

"Yes?" said the doctor patiently.

"It doesn't seem important anymore," she said.

"You've discovered some Venus-flytraps, then?"

"Yes. Aren't they fascinating plants?"

The doctor seemed to be lost in musings. Actually, his old mind was cranking over slowly. Something had been touched. He couldn't quite place it. "Keeping busy, are you?"

"For a head shrinker," Gwen laughed, "you ask a lot of questions. I thought you were just supposed to listen."

"When you're as old as I am, you get impatient," he said. "Especially when your patients won't talk unless primed."

"I've never been accused of not talking enough," she laughed.

"But about what?" He lit a long cigarette and took it to his mouth, shortened it with a long, deep drag. "Not about shotguns in the living room."

"You do get to the heart of things," she said, suddenly uncomfortable. "Would you believe that I was going to clean it for George?"

"No."

She'd been mostly successful at blocking out the entire afternoon. Satan, under observation in the animal hospital, was only days away from freedom and she just days away from what she knew to be a false delivery from a rabies scare. The cat had been inoculated against the disease. Moreover, she knew why he'd attacked her. He had been protecting her. It was grossly unfair to put him in prison for fourteen days for having saved her life. Yet, without telling the entire story she could not get him out. She'd make it up to him. Half and half instead of milk. Fresh hamburger. Poor Satan.

King was looking at her thoughtfully. She shifted in her seat and composed herself. It seemed, now, that she had had a moment of temporary insanity. It was past. She'd had only one nightmare since the event. She was not so weak that she needed to soothe her conscience by confession. Wonderful as George was, he was human, and male. He could not possibly understand that her strange behavior had hurt her far worse than it could ever hurt him. So, she decided, let the hurt be confined.

"It's silly," she said. "I heard something. You know, we're a long way from anyone. I heard what I thought was someone walking on the deck. I got George's gun, then peeked out the door. There was no one, of course."

"Why didn't you say that at first?"

"I don't know," she said. "I suppose I was so upset by poor Satan's insanity—when they possessed him—" She paused, shook her head. "Now why did I say that?"

"Why, do you suppose?"

"I have no idea, but that's what I mean about sounding like someone else."

"Who are they?"

"Dr. King, I have no idea why I said that. I'm not superstitious. I'm not being secretly bewitched by some black magic cult or anything. There's nothing mysterious about me. I just say things out of context, not even realizing I'm saying them." She smiled disarmingly. "I'm just losing a few marbles, not the whole bag."

"Don't try to beat me out of my job, not after thirty-five years," King said, smiling. "I'll make the opinions, if you don't mind, and now my opinion is that it's time for my nap."

When Gwen was gone, he sat heavily on the corner of his office assistant's desk. "You've read the notes on this case?"

"I don't read them, I just type them," she said. Ruth Henley had been Dr. King's assistant for thirty-five years. Once, long ago, before the fires were banked in both of them, she'd shared his bed.

"There's something about it," King said. "I can't put my finger on it. Something which should be right here." He banged on his forehead with his palm.

"I'm having Cornish game hen tonight," Ruth said. "I can fix two as easily as one."

"Nice of you," King said absently. He thunked his thumb nail against his dentures. "Ruthie, when you're not busy—" she snorted "—could you dig back a few years? Something to do with talking to plants, I'd think."

"Any suggestions where to start?" she asked, rising, tucking in her blouse over her old, lax stomach muscles.

"Early, I'd say. Otherwise I'd remember."

"Huh, you forgot where you parked the car the other day." She closed her desk drawer with a thump and looked at her watch. "And you're an hour past due for your heart pill."

"Ummm," he said absently, as she walked stiffly to the water cooler, drew a cup, and brought it to him, extending the vial of small pills. "Yes, definitely something to do with plants. I'd start, if I were you, with the old files."

"You know the dust closes up my sinuses."

"We all have our little crosses to bear," King said, heading for a nap on the big, black couch in his office.

9

It was too hot to clear brush. Moreover, the mosquito crop was a bumper one, and large, yellow, vicious deer flies added to the misery of being outside. Burning citronella torches and a hand fogger made the balcony just barely useable in the late evening. There, over tall gin and tonics, they watched dragonflies flit over the pond and threw peanuts to the friendly squirrels. George had arranged his work schedule to leave Fridays, Saturdays and Sundays free. On weekends they fished. George had worked on every piece of electronic gear in Ocean City, it seemed, and sometimes he took out his pay in a fishing trip to the deep, green waters near the continental shelf, where huge king mackerel and flashing dolphin made for some exciting moments.

In early July, he repaired some small malfunction in an aircraft radio and was invited to take a spin around the area. He called Gwen, who drove the pick-up truck to the airport and joined him, taking the back seat in a sleek Bonanza. From the air, the most impressive thing about the island beach complex was the water. Next, the widespread activity connected with the construction of the atomic generating plant. Huge swatches of earth had been denuded. Around the plant itself, hundreds of acres of woodland had been swept clean by the bulldozers. The cooling canal pointed a bare, straight line toward the waterway, halted there. On the ocean side, a breach had been made in the dunes. The huge spoil area, almost ready to begin to receive the dredged muck from the marsh, was a tremendous gash in the earth, bare, ugly, holding blue-green water in the depths of the main trench.

But the islands were beautiful, looking clean and fresh from the heights. It was a lazy day and the pilot had nothing else to do. The air was smooth and there were no clouds. "You two in any hurry to get back?" he asked, swinging the plane upriver. The marshlands seemed to be mostly water. The lines of demarcation between grass and water clear, hard. The water itself was transparent from the air, showed shell beds, dark spots, a sunken small boat.

"Not at all," George said.

George and the pilot talked technical terms about radios and electronic gear. Gwen's ears cracked and popped as the plane climbed. She could see the coast. The Port City was up ahead. The pilot circled the city and turned inland. He was checking out electronic equipment. The earth below was veined with roads, streams, railroads, and power lines which took huge cuts through dark, green woodlands. Gwen was saddened by the amount of clearing. She wished idly for the opportunity to travel in time, to go back and see the land as it was when the virgin forests covered it. The neat squares of farmland seemed intrusive.

As the aircraft droned onward, they approached an area of small lakes. Scattered, some almost interlocking, they were of curiously similar shape. "They're all round," Gwen said.

"Great," George said. He and the pilot had been ignoring her.

"The lakes are all the same shape," Gwen said.

The pilot twisted his head, throwing his words back toward her as she sat in the rear seat. "They say they were blasted out in a meteorite shower. Actually, they're not all round. More egg-shaped. But in general they're like shell craters, a hole blasted out by an explosion."

"Isn't that funny?" Gwen asked. "Our pond is shaped like them."

"Ours would have been a dinky little meteorite,"

George said. "We should have put in our order for a bigger one, then we'd have a lake big enough to water ski on."

"I'll hop back a few million years and steer you a good one in," Gwen said.

"Now, on this frequency," the pilot said, switching the subject, "we get—"

Gwen, dismissed from man talk, contented herself with looking. The plane was making a bank. Soon she saw the ocean. A cloud bank was building far out.

That night, showers moved in from the sea with thunder and spectacular sheets of lightning. They watched the storms from the living room over gin and tonic, piled onto the rug. George topped off the evening with the Casadesus family playing Papa George's *Concerto for Three Pianos and String Orchestra.* The air conditioner was laboring. It was cool enough, however, to cuddle, without sheets. Gwen slept in a pajama top, George in full-color nudity.

The dream was back, in altered form. The pain was a rending one, not a swift, cutting pain. It was brutal, all-powerful. She fought it in her mind, tried to overcome, could not even awaken and thus drive it away. Behind the pain, the rending, tearing, brutal power, was something new, an awareness, a wistful memory almost touchable, but not quite. Waking, finally, she tried to analyze it. Her memory held tantalizing glimpses of a parklike expanse, of growing things, but nothing she could identify. Strange. A feeling of eternal peace.

The dream became recurrent. First there was raging pain, and then that glimpse of heaven and peace. She was still having the dream when she kept her next appointment with Dr. King. She did not mention it. Instead, feeling that she had to give him something, she talked about her mother. "Ah," he kept saying, his Freudian nature gratified. He felt that at last they were getting down to it. "Ah, ah, I see. Why, do you suppose? Yes. Go on, please."

George had come with her this time. She'd asked that her appointment be changed, for that week only, to Friday, since he needed to make a trip to the city for supplies. He came in just as the interview was over. Ruth, the white-clad, wrinkled nurse with the silvery hair, said, "They're finished. You can go on in."

Gwen and Dr. King were talking about the next appointment. George, not wanting to interrupt, walked around the office and spotted something in his field. "Fantastic machine," he said, when the appointment time was settled and Gwen was gathering her purse and straightening her skirt.

"Oh?" said King. "You're familiar with a polygraph?"

"Not really," George said. "I've read a bit about them."

"King's folly," the doctor said. "An expensive toy. It hasn't worked since I bought it." He chuckled. "Of course, my experiments with it so far have been with myself and with my office nurse." He brushed at his vest. "Perhaps we don't get good readings because we're both so old we have no blood pressure."

"I understand that the operation has a lot to do with the operator's knowledge," George said innocently. "Not that I'm saying you don't know how to operate it."

King chuckled again. "You may be right. But I do think there's a malfunction. I'm waiting for the factory man to come. He makes regular trips to the area to service the various police gadgets, but trying to get him to make a special trip is, I've found, impossible."

"My husband can fix anything electronic," Gwen said.

"Oh?"

"Well, I don't know anything about this particular machine," George said.

"My main interest is in the movements of electrodermal currents," King said. "I bought this expensive toy thinking that I would prove some theories I have regarding emotions. But the electrodes here give absolutely no readings."

"Well," George said, "the principle behind the thing is simple. If I had the schematics—"

"I think, yes," King said, digging into a drawer, coming up with a thick book of electrical diagrams. "If these mean anything to you."

George thumbed through them and found the one he wanted. He furrowed his brow in thought. "Couldn't be but one or two things," he said.

"Young man," King said. "If you could fix this diabolical thing I'd be forever grateful."

"Well, I don't have any equipment here," George said. Gwen could see that he was interested. Being able to put his hands on a new and complicated piece of electronic gear was pure bliss to George.

"Take it with you. It's taking up space, gathering dust. I used to have the couch here." Dr. King gestured. "Where it is now the sun gets in my eyes unless I close the shades."

"In an M.G.?" Gwen laughed.

"I can come over in the pick-up," George said, hooked.

He did. He arose early the next morning, leaving Gwen asleep, with a note on the bedside table. She was awakened late by the growl of the heavy equipment. At first, she thought it was across the waterway, where the cranes and drag lines and earth movers were piling a fifteen-foot-high dike to hold stinking marsh mud. Then she realized that they were closer. She'd had the dream again. She was not refreshed by her night's sleep. She dozed. She awoke, screaming aloud. She had experienced the sensation of having her upper torso twisted and ripped away from her lower body.

Two big Cat bulldozers had been moved onto Pine Tree island. There was plenty of time. Two could do the job nicely, since there was only a half-mile strip of woodland to be cleared. It would take months to dredge the canal across the marsh. The operators were buddies who had worked for the prime contractor of the generating plant for two years, having signed on as heavy equipment operators at a job in Texas. They'd followed the construction jobs since. Billy Daniels was twenty-five and unmarried, a handsome, long-haired, husky kid from Dallas. He liked women, booze, and hunting quail, about in that order. He had a way with all of his pet hobbies. His buddy, Jock Peebles, was a year older, more quiet, but able to kill a fifth of bourbon and still function. Billy was more at ease with the girls, and had lined up both of them with a pair of sisters in Port City. He got into his girl's pants the first night by promising to love her forever and take her with him when the job moved on. There was no real danger in making the promise, because the current job was good for three more years.

Billy and Jock shared a mobile home parked on the far side of Ocean City in a new trailer park. There was an old gal from Tennessee there—married, two kids, husband a welder on the night shift—who had been giving Billy the eye. He had his eye on her, too. He made a ten-dollar bet with Jock that he'd be in her pants within thirty days.

Surveyors had been through before the dozers. The outlines of the cut were there. Bush axes had laid low the brush along the lines, and you could stand on one end of the area and look all the way through along the surveyed lines. Since it takes room to work a big Cat, Jock went crunching inland from the beach road, leaving Billy to start on the edge. Most of the trees were small, and you could push up a helluva pile of them with one straight run. Now and then Billy would come on a biggie, and those he liked. He liked plowing into a huge pine with the blade raised a couple of feet, hitting with a jar which he felt all the way to his balls, the tracks digging and then spinning as the big pine fought back. It was, Billy thought, having undergone the unpleasant experience just a few months back, sort of like a dentist pulling a stubborn wisdom tooth. He had to rock the bastard, pushing and loosening, then the big push and the tree's tap root snapping below ground, sometimes with a crack that he could hear. Then the whole thing would come out, caught on his sharp dozer blade, to topple with a hissing fall, and then a big whooshing crash with limbs breaking and pine cones flying everywhere.

Pushing a Cat was good loot and it paid for a lot of good booze and bought pretties for reluctant women. Billy was good at it. He was better than Jock, and Jock was a damned good Cat man. But Billy could outwork him and did with regularity. In no time, he had a cleared place, raw earth torn, torn roots bleeding sap. He then began to push the fallen trees and brush into the cleared area. After it dried a little, the laborers would come around, douse it with gasoline, and burn it. Fresh-pushed trees were the devil to burn. It took days and a lot of gas to do it.

Billy figured he and Jock could make the job last two weeks, if they paced it. It could have been finished in ten days, but then they'd have to go back over the creek to work with that bastard foreman who, one day, was going to get his teeth altered by Billy's fist. He liked being all alone, just him and Jock in the woods, with the big Cat growling and heating up. Sweat began to soak through his denims, broken branches and pine cones falling clip, clop on the top of his protective cage.

Billy saw the girl just before he was ready to knock off for lunch. He was working automatically in an area of twisted, small oaks, and his mind was on the ham and egg sandwiches in his lunch pail. She was standing on the edge of the growing cut area, under a pine. Her arms were crossed in front of her so that he couldn't tell whether or not she had a good set, but she looked good otherwise. Her hair was neat and done up in one of those sophisticated, simple buns. Her legs, encased in slacks, looked good. He couldn't see her face from that distance, but faces didn't mean too much to him, just so they didn't need a paper sack to put over them. She was still there when he made a turn and pushed a pile of fallen trees into the growing mound at the center of the cut.

He'd been saving a big oak. He'd cleared around it, because it was a monster and would take all the Cat could give. He wanted room to work it. He was used to having people watch him work the Cat. People were fascinated by power. Girls liked dozer operators, maybe because they thought some of that power was transferred to their loins. So he was doing his job and putting on a show at the same time when he rammed the big oak, causing it to shiver to the top of its hundred-year-old mass. Man, it was a mother. It fought and fought, but the power of the big Cat was just too much. The tree dropped a few brittle limbs on him when he hit it hard, the limbs crashing and crunching atop his protective cage, but in the end it went over, with a groan of splintering wood which could be heard over the roar of the big diesel engine. The thing went down on its outstretched limbs. They shattered under the weight of the main trunk. For a while, there it was, crash, crunch, snap. Billy looked over toward where the girl was standing. As he watched, she turned and disappeared into the woods, but not before he saw enough to arouse his interest. Billy was a fanny man. She had a fine one. He didn't say anything about his audience to Jock. Hell, a man can only share so much with his buddy. While he ate he wondered if she had been just a passing tourist or if she lived nearby. He hoped the latter. At any rate, he'd be watching for her.

Gwen had been drawn to the canal cut by the noise and by something else, a nagging sense of something, duty, curiosity, disgust. It was just too nebulous to define, that feeling, but she'd been saddened by what she saw. It reminded her of the air view of the area. Hundreds of acres of former woodland now bare and blowing sand. When the big oak went down, she felt like weeping. A hundred years to grow, outliving generations of man, surviving hurricanes, drought, fire. It took the machine about ten minutes to negate a century of growth. She was moody and hot after her walk through the woods. She walked to the clear pond and pulled off her shoes. The water was delicious on her feet, but she did not even consider a swim. Without George around, the pool looked deep and lonely. George's swimming activity had flattened the tall grass at the edge of the water. She sat down, feeling a slight dampness on her seat. She splashed her feet idly, trying to dispel the gloom. The roar of the heavy equipment, at least of the bulldozers nearest her, was silenced. Nature, however, is never totally silent. She heard birds rustling the leaves in the uncleared areas, a squirrel calling, the caw of a crow, and the lovely trill of a mockingbird. Gradually, a feeling of contentment came over her.

She'd had a nice long session with Dr. King, talking freely about her mother. She decided that she felt better, understood the woman more, although the doctor had not done any more than George had done. He had mainly just allowed her to voice her opinions.

"You know," she told herself, "you've really got it made."

At their age they were unusually secure, thanks to George's father's belief in insurance. George liked his work. They had a beautiful home. There were dark areas in her life, but a monthly show of red had negated one of her most awful worries. She was not pregnant by the meter reader.

It was really unbelievable, that thing that had happened. If she lived to be a hundred, she'd never understand her actions, but there, in the hot sun, with the cool water laving her feet, she no longer felt suicidal about it. Desperately sorry, yes. She thought she'd give her right hand to erase that event. Then she wondered why she'd thought of that particular old bromide. She shook her head. She didn't want to think of unpleasant things, the dreams for example. She felt that she was on the way back and was going to beat it, whatever it was. It was simple to accept the Freudian thing and blame it all on mama.

She had so much that she was not going to throw it away, a great man, a fine life, and all the love she could handle—taking the meaning of the word both ways.

She lay back and covered her eyes with one arm. It was so peaceful there. She was dozing when the bulldozers started work again. The muffled roars caused her to frown. Even that would pass. People had babies and the babies grew up and used electricity. There had to be power plants or the race would go back to cave-man living, and she would not have liked that. She liked having a nice stereo set with records which turned her on, liked the ease of electric cooking and washing and ironing and all that. It would pass. She pushed the engine sounds into the back of her mind and tried to regain that drowsy sense of well-being.

She thought of the island as it once was, wild, huge trees never touched by saw or ax. The trees would have closed off the floor of the forest from the sun, and there, underneath a shady canopy, would be only a thick mulch of pine straw and leaves, clear, cool. It was a nice thought. She'd never seen a virgin forest, only second-growth timber with thick underbrush and weedy plants. She imagined the forest of three hundred years past and then, further than that, back through the eons to ages of giant ferns and strange, lumbering animals.

Something crawled on her foot. She kicked and looked down. A pulpy tentacle of the water plant which covered the bottom of the pond had drifted across her instep. She stretched, her heels in the very edge of the water, and yawned. The sun felt so good, the water so cool. An image. She, like a plant, head lifted to the sun, feet, roots, in cool, wet earth. She dug her feet into the wet sand, sighed with the feel of it. What would she be? A rose? A giant sequoia? Or that desert tree which lived thousands, wasn't it, of years? A rose was glamorous, but there were all sorts of things that ate it. A tree. Sequoia. Hundreds of years old. A line from a song, "and if you could speak, what a fascinating tale you could tell." She would want some defense, however, so that when the loggers came she could drop a limb on their heads. Well, they'd just build cages to protect them, like the bulldozer operator.

Idle mind, idle thoughts, she told herself, thinking about going inside to have a bite of something or to paint. But she was so lazy.

There is a delicious feeling of contentment when one falls asleep slowly for a practice nap. As she shaded her eyes from the sun with one arm, she thought, If I could be this sleepy when I go to bed I'd never dream. Pure luxury. Letting the eyes close, the lids so heavy, so heavy. And half-sleep, an awareness of sounds, but as if they came from a distance. Comfort. Lazy comfort. Peace. Around her the living things were known, friendly, and symbiotic. Shared things, the perfume of flowers, the rich fruit given freely, she, herself, knowing the goodness of the rich earth, yet mobile, returning to it for health and sustenance. At the end of the day planting herself, coming back to the rich earth. Feeding. An absence of pain and fear. It was a beautiful dream and it was real and the landscape was eerily familiar, yet strange.

She felt heavy and ripe. It was a good, natural feeling. A bee buzzed on a weed flower near her ear. Birds called, and a mosquito whined near her head but did not bite. She sat up, feeling languidly at peace. Her clothes constrained her. She loosened her blouse and left it open to the waist. The sun felt good on her bare skin. She wore a small, natural-feel tricot bra. She felt like saying, "Yum," when she breathed the air, it was so pure, so delicately flavored with the sweet oxygen given off by the growing things around her.

A noise at the far end of the pond caused her to turn her head, not in panic, in interest, slowly. Sam started barking. Two teen-age boys came out of the brush, did not see her, halted to look at the pond. Ripe, swollen, heavy. Good, natural. She stretched, pushing out her breasts. She raised a hand, waved at them. They saw and waved back hesitantly.

"Come here," she called, just loudly enough to be heard.

They consulted, moved slowly around the pond. She waited, ripe, mellow, natural.

"No." She heard it deep inside, a small voice. "No." That part of her knew, recognized the feeling of ripeness. That part of her screamed, protested. The two boys, tall, lithe, and handsome, moved toward her, walking slowly around the far end of the clear pond.

"I won't," she whispered. "I will not."

She was talking to someone or something. She couldn't see or hear that someone or that something, but it was there. "I won't."

"Yes, yes," the very air seemed to be saying. "Yes," inside her. Open yourself here, naturally, on the grass.

They were fifty yards away, nearing her. She shook her head, fighting the conflicting desires, the ripe, natural, sweet want versus the agony of knowledge. If she yielded to her impulses, she could not live with herself.

Sam, barking, escorted them. Her stomach and her scantily covered breasts were exposed. They could see. "No, please," she begged. "No."

There was an alternative. It was so frightening that she screamed, the sound shrill, harsh, breaking the silence. The two boys halted. The alternative was presented again, vividly. She screamed anew, and the two boys broke into a run and crashed away into the brush. She stood, breathing hard, tears wetting her face. "No," she said. "Oh, no."

Then, in sudden contrast, the scene of pure bliss, endless peace, immortality, heaven. Strange, lovely landscape. The moment of terror was wiped away. It was if it had never happened. She saw and understood. She had a choice, but that choice did not include inactivity. As if to drive home the point, she was swept with unbearable agony, terminal agony, twisted, torn, and rended, her limbs being shattered. It was only a moment, but in that terrifying moment she saw more and understood more and knew, with regret and a sweet, unreachable sadness, what she must do.

A quick summer shower crossed the island as George came home. As he entered the drive, the windshield wipers making rhythmic sweeps, he saw Gwen, her blouse open, her hair wet and streaming down her back, standing down by the pond. He was dry, but he would have to change from his work clothes anyhow. It was a warm, pleasant summer shower, so he ran through it and yelped at her. She turned around and smiled.

"Hi, nuthead," he said, gathering her into his arms. "Why the rain act?"

"It feels good, doesn't it?" Rain ran down her face. She licked at it with her tongue. "I haven't walked in the rain in, oh, years."

"Ever screwed in the rain?" He pinched her breast through the wet tricot bra which showed the outline of a nipple.

"No. You?"

"Come to think of it, no." He was grinning. He was

pleased. She looked better, happier, more herself than she had in weeks.

"Well?" she asked, giving him her sexiest look.

"You're kidding."

"All show and no go," she said.

"A Ferrier never lets a dare go by," he said, starting to strip the sodden clothing away from her.

Her healthy skin beaded the rain at first. He looked at her, entranced. His Gwen, the nut, the prude, was naked in the open, laughing in the rain. "Honey?" he asked. The sight of her turned him on.

"Yes," she whispered through the rain. "Yes, darling."

He couldn't believe it. He made a mental note to leave his fortune to the study of psychiatry. He blessed Dr. Irving King as she clung and pulled. He giggled as he arranged their sodden clothing on the grass, and then it was a serious, beautiful thing, with a wildly responsive, willing, wanton woman, wanton just for him, loving his touch, and saying, "Ah, ah, ah," with his penetration. George was a happy man. The union was quick, total, violently active. Finished, he saw love and laughter in her eyes, felt his own laugh overflowing.

"God, you're silly," she said, pushing him off and running, with him giving chase, to splash noisily into the rain-dimpled clear pond.

Inside, after a hot shower, a mutual rubdown with rough towels, a drink, and music on the player, he wondered if it were only a momentary release on her part, if she'd go back. As if in answer, she came to him, crawling into his lap as he sat in the big, gold chair. "George?"

"Ummm."

"George." A whisper, a sensual kiss on his cheek, a hand doing things Gwen's hands had never done.

"Hey, am I in the right place?" He cringed. He shouldn't have said it.

"You're different."

"Like it?"

"God, yes."

He liked it. He liked it. His Gwen, the wanton, sexy, endlessly hungry woman. As the days went by and things didn't change, he began to hope. At first, when indulging an old whim, such as making love in the big chair, he'd say, "Are you sure?" Then he forgot to ask. It was a fantastic week. George loved his new wife more than he'd ever, ever loved the old one. He was a happy man and she was happy and uninhibited and loving.

"I just don't understand," he said, making one last try to figure it out.

"I don't either, really. It just came to me. All of a sudden I said, Gwen, that's me, you know, you're a big girl. He's your husband and he loves you. Give, baby." She giggled. "I find giving to be, frankly, one hell of a lot of fun."

So he accepted it and was happy. He would be one happy fellow right up to the day he died.

10

Billy was working the inland side of the cut. Jock, his friend, was on the ocean side. There was a buildup of clouds to the west, indicating a short work day. Billy was rooting for the clouds. He'd had a rough night. First, he and Jock had stopped by a joint in Ocean City on the way home, punched a few coins into the juke for a couple of country-western goodies, shot a few games of bowling on the little game machine, and put away a few tall, cold Buds. Back at the trailer, Billy had been restless. Jock was out of it. He could hold his booze, but beer did him in and made him sleepy. He hit the sack just after dark, leaving Billy on his own. He considered calling the two sisters, and entertained a delightful vision of talking both of them into bed at one time. He had to walk all the way to the office to use the telephone. The aged, short, fat, wrinkled mother of the two sisters answered and said, rather curtly, that her daughters were not in. Billy said to hell with it and walked back down the line of trailers, kicking at the bare, white sand.

The Tennessee girl came out of her trailer just as he was out front. She had her bleached hair piled up high in a beehive. She wore slacks which showed the outline of her panties and the firmness of her fanny. Jesus, she was a piece.

"Evenin'," Billy said, giving her his best smile.

"Hi yawl, Billy." She was walking right toward him, her big set bouncing inside a little knit thing.

"Where you off to?" he asked, seeing that she was headed toward her new Ford. He stood in front of the car door to block her.

"Outta cigarettes," she said. She was, he could tell, well aware of the fact that he was looking toward her with more than neighborly interest.

"Your old man get off to work?"

"Damn night shift," she said.

"Might ride along with you, if you don't mind," Billy said.

She looked around. The evening was a hot one and everyone was inside, window air conditioners were roaring and pumping. "Well, I'm just going down to the store."

He walked around and got in. He saw, when she sat down, that he'd been wrong. She had on a bra, after all. She just had a set so big that no bra could handle them, that was all. She smelled of a nice perfume and—before the air conditioner beat down the accumulated heat in the car—a bit of good girl sweat.

The nearest store was on the outskirts of Ocean City,

five or six miles up the road. Billy began his work immediately. "Don't you get lonesome all by yourself every night?"

"You don't have time to get lonesome with kids," she said.

"Shame for a good-looking girl like you to spend every evening with no more company than a couple of kids," he said.

"Breaks of the game," she said, but she turned her face toward him with a quick smile.

Billy talked a little trash, and she was giving all the right answers. When they got to the little service station and grocery store, he said he'd go in. She gave him a dollar for two packs of Camel filters, and he came out with a cold six-pack. He went first class, because she was a pretty classy broad. He bought one of those expensive brands.

"Christ, yeah," she said. "Hit the spot."

She drove with the cold bottle between her legs. Billy didn't want to cool off that spot. He had other ideas.

"Seen the dig lately?" He was referring to the huge excavation for the base of the reactors.

"Naw."

"Let's drive in and take a look," he said.

"Sam sees me riding around with you, it'll be him and you," she said.

"He don't have to see us," he said, smiling. He pointed to a little lumber road as they approached it. "Take a right."

She did. His heart started pumping. He killed his beer and twisted the cap off another. She hadn't finished hers. He reached for it to test it and then, finding it half full, pushed it back down, with a little twisting motion, between her legs. The road ended at a temporary fence. "Can't see much from here," she said, lifting her beer after throwing the car into park, leaving the motor running. Billy reached across and turned off the key and doused the lights.

"Good view," he said. In front of them the tall buildings were floodlit. There wasn't a blade of grass, not a single runty tree between the fence and the installation. On one of the projects, sparks flew from an electric welder.

"That's where Sam works," she said.

"Yeah." He moved in. When he pressed his flank up against hers she made a small motion to move away. She didn't have any place to go. He put his arm around her and put his other hand on her chin and pulled her face toward him. "I've been looking at you for a long time," he said.

"I don't mind looking, buster," she said, "but that's the end of it."

"Be nice," he said, kissing her. She went all wet and open, her tongue coming out. Then she jerked away.

"You crazy or something?"

"Crazy for you," Billy said, trying to put his mouth on hers again.

"Knock it off," she said. "I'm a married woman."

"I won't let that bother me if you won't let it bother you," he said, trying to put his hand on her and finding that she had six arms to ward him off.

"Sam would kill you," she said, fighting.

"You gonna tell him?"

"There ain't gonna be nothing to tell," she said, ramming an elbow into his gut, hard.

"Ouch," he said.

"You get over there and stay," she said.

"Now, honey," he said.

"I'm leaving," she said harshly. "You wanta ride home you can, but you keep your ass on your side of the automobile."

"You gonna waste a beautiful opportunity like this?" He tried to put his arms around her. She hit into his belly with her closed fist.

"Goddamnit, that hurt," he said.

"Get you where it really hurts if you don't stop acting like a animal."

"Animal?" He felt the heat of anger. "Animal?"

She started the car. He had this huge want and she'd promised him. Her earlier actions had been a promise. She'd led him on and now she was showing her true colors. A tease. That's all she was.

"You know you want to," he said, making one last effort.

"I won't deny it," she said. He reached for her as she started the engine. "But I've got enough sense for my wants not to hurt me, and yours are going to get you hurt if you don't get your hands off me."

"You want to," he persisted.

She drove home in silence, and he let his anger vent off by closing the door with a crash when he got out. So it was one hell of a frustrating night. She wanted to but she wouldn't. The way it was with most women, damn it.

He was still thinking about it when he saw the girl come out onto the edge of the cut. He'd been watching the clouds hopefully. If it rained he could quit and go into Ocean City and try his luck at the joint with that tall waitress. When a man is desperate, he's desperate and if there'd been an organized house in the little town he'd have made plans to visit it that very night, but all Ocean City had was a couple of part-time hookers, and they didn't look too clean to him. He wasn't about to waste twenty bucks on something which might begin chewing on him before he even got finished.

Then the girl was there and she was in an outfit that knocked his eyes out. Hotpants and a low-necked blouse. He could see, even from fifty yards away, that she didn't have a set as big as the Tennessee gal, but she was making up for that with a pair of legs which looked good and that nice fanny. He kept his eyes on her. When she waved, he waved back. She stood there for a long time. The low clouds climbed the sky, building.

"Nothing ventured," he said. He cut the Cat's engine, leaving the blade up, ready to go back to work. He walked over the torn ground, lifting his boots over roots and broken limbs.

"Hey," he said, "you look mighty lonesome out here all by yourself." Close up, she had a knock-out of a face.

"This way," she said, turning without so much as a smile. He saw her fanny work as she walked away. What the hell? She stopped, turned. "Are you coming?"

"Where?" he asked.

"Does it matter?" she asked, turning to face him and unbuttoning her blouse to show that she was wearing nothing under it. She let it hang open, showing a nice, firm set. Tender stuff.

"Honey, you name the place."

He'd heard of such things, but nothing like this had ever happened to him. He almost stumbled over his third leg as he followed her down into the brush along a little trail. It was hot in the woods, with the breeze blocked off. He didn't care. Man, after his disappointment of the night before, he was ready. And he couldn't believe his luck, but he'd heard of such things, women so hot they didn't beat around the bush. He followed. She skirted a little bay. The clouds were still coming. The sun went, and it cooled down. She pushed through thick brush and he fell back so that the bent branches wouldn't snap up into his face. When he broke through she was standing beside a big tree which had been blown over in some past storm.

"Stand over there and take off your clothes," she said, pointing toward the root end of the fallen tree, a huge mass of dirt and moss and rotting wood. She didn't beat around the bush. To show that he was up to anything, he stepped over. The place where the tree had been growing was a big, round hole about four feet deep. There was water standing in the bottom of the hole. Billy wondered where she was going to do it. There wasn't enough moss anywhere to make a good carpet. Hell, he didn't care. Looking at her bare boobs, he was hot enough to screw her standing up against the tree, even if it did tire his legs and make them tremble.

"Take off your clothes," she said. She wasn't smiling. Billy began to wonder if this were some sort of a con. He looked around. There were no sounds, save the natural sounds of a woodland.

"You first," he said. He wasn't born yesterday. If this was something some of the guys had set up for a laugh, he'd go along, but he'd see the rest of her, even if they did come busting out and start laughing. Then he'd have something.

She nodded, shed the blouse in one graceful motion, loosened her hotpants, let them fall. She had a thick, brown bush and sweet-looking legs. She kicked the hotpants aside. Billy's throat was dry. He took a step toward her. She said, "Now you."

He grinned. This was surely the real thing. A real nymph, and those psychos were always hung-up about something, even if they did make good rocking when they got started. He took off his shirt and hung it over the fallen tree. Then he had to take off his boots. His jeans were so tight they wouldn't come off over the boots. He bent and tugged, and off came one boot. Then he lifted the other foot, lost his balance, and caught himself with one hand on the fallen tree. He laughed nervously. He'd taken his eyes off her for only a few seconds. When he looked up, he looked into the barrel of a shotgun. The woman was moving closer.

"Oh, shi—" The spreading pattern of shot blasted the last letter of the word down his throat before tearing off the lower side of his face. The second blast eliminated his eyes. He splashed heavily into the hole.

Gwen padded over to look down on him. She sidestepped the bloody leaves. He jerked a few times and then was still. She leaned the shotgun up against the fallen tree and calmly began to push the bloodied leaves into the hole with a stick. Finished, she examined her work critically. There were a couple of blood spots on the tree itself. She cupped her hand, dug dirt after pushing the mulch aside, and rubbed the tree until the spots were obliterated. She looked at her dirtied hand, wiped it on leaves, and dressed slowly. Then, using shells taken from a small bag hidden in the dead branches of the tree, she reloaded the gun and placed it in its original spot.

Jock, Billy's best friend, stopped his Cat. The clouds were on top of him and it was time to knock off. He heard only silence and knew that Billy had decided the same thing. He sighed, stretched, and lit a cigarette. He sat on the Cat waiting, and after five minutes got off and took a long, satisfying leak. Pushing a Cat worked on the kidneys. Then he started walking around the remaining mass of trees toward the other end to meet Billy. He walked all the way to Billy's machine and saw Billy's tracks leading off toward the woods. He was headed toward them when the girl came out from under the trees.

"Hi," she said.

"Hi." She was some looker. "You seen the guy running that dozer?"

"Ummm," she said. There was a teasing little smile on her face. Jock couldn't believe what he was seeing and what he was thinking. Billy was a real cocksman, but this wasn't Billy's kind of chick. This one was high-class stuff.

"I saw him," she said, with what amounted to a knowing smirk. "He said I should see you, too. He said you would be nice."

Once in Dallas Jock had taken seconds on one of Billy's girls, a kid who just couldn't get enough. He was a true believer. Still, there was something about this girl. "You pulling my leg?"

"He's down there waiting," she said. "He asked me to come and get you."

That damned Billy. Only man Jock knew who could find a piece in the middle of the woods on the job. He followed, his interest growing. The girl didn't talk any more, but she spoke with the swing of her hips. Jock followed her down a little trail into thick brush and then into a small clearing beside a fallen tree. "Where's Billy?" he asked.

"I told him I didn't want an audience." She was opening her blouse. Jock's throat constricted. He moved toward her.

"No," she said sharply. "I want you to take off your clothes first."

"This some kind of gag?" Jock asked.

"Is it?" She dropped her hotpants, and he licked his lips and began to move toward her again.

"No," she said. "I want to watch you undress."

"You do it for me, honey," he said, moving.

"Humor me," she said. "I have a thing about it."

He halted. She was just a few steps away, the hotpants down around her ankles. As he watched, she kicked them aside. She was nude, lovely, soft, all woman. "Stand over there where I can see."

He did. He hung his shirt on the tree and bent to take off his boots, and he didn't even look up.

By pushing the accumulated dirt from the overhanging roots, she was able to cover them. She put their loose clothing under the top one and then pushed the dirt in and then pushed away leaves and got down to sand and used a stick to dig and push until there was a layer of dirt a foot deep atop them and all the nooks formed by tangled legs and arms were filled in. Then she covered the whole thing with leaves and, dressed, gathered pine straw to cover the entire clearing so as to hide the foot marks.

Then she examined it carefully for blood and other signs and, satisfied, skirted the bay, gained the road, and walked slowly and tiredly to the house. There she got out the gun cleaning kit and scoured the barrels of the gun. She oiled it, put it away, and showered. It had begun to rain, a hard downpour which, she knew, would settle the freshly raked leaves in the clearing and eliminate all traces of her having been there. It was Friday. The machines would sit all weekend in the raw, ugly cut. On Monday, there would be no one to run them. That, she knew, was only a temporary condition. There would be others. There would be many others. Too many. But for a time, at least, the pain was lessened.

She spent the rest of the afternoon sitting in the big room, watching the rain fall on the small shoots which were once again sprouting up in George's cleared areas. Now and then, as if she'd heard something pleasing, she'd nod and smile.

II

It was one of the most beautiful weekends in George's life. Hot, Jesus, it was hot. He spent Friday working, on one of his regular days off, getting out a couple of rush jobs, and then finding it surprisingly simple to repair Dr. King's polygraph. Just a bad wiring job. A cold solder joint. He traced the circuit, found the break, and cleaned off the bad joint. Then he soldered it and hooked up the gadget, after reading a few pages of instructions to a high school kid who liked to hang around and talk electronics. The electrodes were registering the movement of electrical currents on the skin, and George was pleased. He carried the machine home and put it in the big room.

There was a movie on in Port City which had received

good reviews and was, seemingly, headed for Academy Awards. It was about a tough cop who called a spade a spade. George, a true Southerner, cringed when he read something about "a black from Alabama." "Blacks," to him, were primitive natives of some British colonial country. "I say, old bean, the blacks are restless tonight." All that sort of rot. He thought the movie to be refreshing because it called crime crime even when performed by a "black." George believed in law and order for everyone, saying after the movie, that laws held civilization together, defining civilization as those things which made him comfortable, relatively knowledgeable, and free to do things which pleased him as long as he did not infringe on other people's freedoms. The movie also pleased him with its direct approach to the drug problem.

"That cop wouldn't vote for legalization of marijuana," he told Gwen.

"We never needed drugs," Gwen said dreamily. She was snuggled in her bucket seat, her head back, listening to George with half an ear. "The air itself was wine."

"Boy," he said.

"I'm sorry. I was sort of daydreaming," she said, sitting up straight and touching his leg. "You must think I'm a real nut."

"Think?" He laughed. "Honey, I know." He put his arm around her, and pulled her close—as close as you can pull a girl in a bucket-seat sports car. "But I love you."

"Please go on loving me, George." The urgency in her voice touched him. "I need you now, more than ever."

"You've got me, kid."

She had him. It was wild and exciting and very athletic. He zonked off into sleep and woke to a perfect Saturday. She was bright and cheerful. The heavy equipment across the waterway was working, but the machines were down into sterile earth, digging bare sand and piling it into dikes around the long, raw pit. He read the paper at breakfast, ate too much, and worked the crossword puzzle while she cleared the table. They walked their "estate." George remarked that he should get around to clearing paths and buying those horses. Gwen said she had all the animals she could take care of, what with Sam and the new Pup. She very carefully, as usual, avoided mention of Satan. The cat, cleared of the bum rap of rabies, had found a nice home on a dairy farm in the adjoining county.

The wild flytraps at the boggy end of the clear pond were seeding. Their traps were healthy, red, and voracious. The inside plants were equally healthy. Gwen decided, although the plants propagated best from root stock, to try some seeds. George watched her gather some of the eggplant-shaped seeds and said, "Those things have a fascination for you, huh?"

"They're unusual."

"That I know. They grow only in this small coastal section."

"Yes."

"Interesting to speculate why," George said.

"The soil is acid," Gwen said.

"This isn't the only acid soil in the world."

"They don't like to be too far from—" She didn't finish.

"From what?"

"Oh, I don't really know." She walked away toward the house.

"How did they get the name Venus-flytrap?" George asked, catching up with her.

"Obvious," she said. "They're from Venus."

"Sure." He swatted her on her well-padded fanny. "And in the books, it's Venus's-flytrap, anyhow, indicating that they were named after the goddess, not the planet."

"There is a connection even there," Gwen said. "Venus was not exactly of this earth."

"You are one spooky broad." George laughed. She glanced at him, her eyes hooded.

Inside, she stored the seeds. George stripped and put on a bathing suit. "Come for a swim?"

"I'll watch."

He hit the water on the run, knifed into it, splashed, swam, and bellowed at Gwen, who sat on the balcony. She had gin and tonic ready when he came dripping his way onto the deck. "Before the sun crosses the yardarm?" he asked.

Pleasantly potted, he moved speakers to the balcony, juiced the amp up to three-quarters volume, and blasted the woodland with the choral movement from Beethoven's *Ninth*. There was a breeze to blow away bugs. Gwen danced to "Turkish Bath," after George had his fill of grandeur and went into something that just sat there and swung. After the walk in the woods, she'd changed to hotpants and the effect of her energetic belly dance was a good one on George. He smoked, enjoying the cigarette as only a cigarette can be enjoyed after a few tall ones, clapped, urged her on, and repeated the selection. He forced her to dance until she was laughing and panting.

Late evening. Unexpected company in the form of Peter Braws, his wife, and a nice young couple, relatives of Mrs. Braws. The bring-your-own-bottle politeness of the guests put plenty of booze in the house, and the party went on until late hours with loud music, laughter, and good feelings.

Sunday morning. Waking to find Gwen's soft, moist, warm body draped over his. A slow, lingering morning love making and breakfast, with gallons of tomato juice and a quick swim and the sun and Gwen in a laughing mood. Sunday papers on the balcony in the breeze. "I think I'll clear the beach for you." George said, feeling the need for exercise after too much booze the night before.

"No." The sharpness of it startled him. He looked at her inquiringly. "Not today," she said, smiling. "I don't want you out of my sight today."

"I'll just be right down below."

"Out of reach, then," she said, coming to him. When her intentions became clear, he groaned in mock agony.

"You're going to wear me out."

She did mischief with her hands and lips. "Complaining?"

"That'll be the day," he said.

A thousand years of it wouldn't be enough. It was a thoroughly beautiful weekend. When the bugs began to take advantage of the evening's lull, they went inside. George worked at a crossword puzzle. Gwen fed the flytraps raw hamburger. George looked up and noticed the rapt look on her face. "I told you that when those nasty little bastards started turning you on they'd have to go." He wasn't interested in the puzzle. He rose to watch her. He passed by the polygraph. As he watched a flytrap close rapidly on a morsel of hamburger he had a thought. "It's electrical, I'd guess. I wonder if it could be measured?" He set up the machine. Gwen stopped her feeding process and watched. When he started to hook the electrodes onto the flytrap she stopped him.

"You're not going to hurt it?"

"It's not alive, Gwen. Not in that sense."

"Don't hurt it."

"So, O.K., I won't hurt the little bastard."

He attached the electrodes gently. "Now, what I want to see," he said, making adjustments, "is if the electric current registers when the trap closes. You drop in the hamburger."

The polygraph recorder leaped. "Something wrong," he said. Gwen dropped the bit of meat and the trap closed. There was a strong reading of current. "I'll be damned," he said. He moved the electrodes to another plant and Gwen stood ready. "Now," he said. "Shit." For there was another surge, just as he'd said "now," with the image of her dropping the hamburger into the trap in his mind. The movement of electronic current registered, too. He didn't begin to suspect until the process had been repeated several times. In each case, his thoughts of feeding the plant, his mental image, stimulated a reading much like that of a person showing emotional stimulation.

"The bastards are reading my mind," he said. He had the electrodes connected to a different plant. "That's crazy."

"I don't know," Gwen said.

"Watch this." George reached for a knife from the cabinet. He held it behind him and approached the flytrap that was wired to the polygraph. "I'm going to cut you into tiny pieces," he said. The recorder leaped, stuttered, and then began to draw a straight line on the paper. "Sonofabitch," George said. He reached out his hand and mutilated the trap, crushing it between his fingers. The action of the polygraph went unnoticed, for Gwen screamed and began to hit him on the shoulders, yelling, "No, no, stop it." He didn't notice the recordings of the graph until he'd calmed her. At the moment of his mutilation, the recorder had gone wild.

"I'm sorry," Gwen said. "It's just that I've grown fond of them."

"This is too spooky for me," he said. "The bastard reads my mind. It faints when I threaten it. It goes crazy when it's hurt."

"Let's leave them alone," Gwen said.

"And you, going ape on me." He grinned. "In love with a Venus-flytrap?"

"Silly."

"But it's damned interesting, isn't it?"

"Yes."

"Let's try something else." He hooked up to an African violet. The plant was due for water. He reached for a glass, ran it full, and started to pour. The reaction was much weaker, but there was a reaction, a movement of the recording stylus, before he started watering the plant. And when he thought an image of fire, of burning a leaf of the lush plant, the "fainting" reaction was there. The stylus leaped, as when a human being shows emotional distress, and then it leveled off into a straight line.

George had a new interest. First thing Monday morning, he was in the yard, the polygraph hooked into a tree. He stroked the tree with his hand. He threatened it with an ax. Since it was one which had been slated to be cleared, he drove the sharp blade into the wood and then watched, grim-faced, as the pain reaction sent the recording stylus dancing.

"This is crazy," he told a watching Gwen.

"I could have told you."

"If I believe this, I can never mow a lawn, clear brush, cut firewood, trim bushes. Hell, I won't even be able to eat greens. This bastard fainted when I came at it with an ax."

"You're beginning to understand," Gwen said softly.

"Not at all," he said.

He did some reading. He found that his discovery was not original. There'd been work done in the polygraph field with plants, and the results were the same as his own. The pioneer in the work, Cleve Backster, even used the same words, saying that plants "fainted" when threatened. Backster, he found, had some pretty heavy thoughts regarding plants. His work, according to printed reports, showed that plants appreciated being watered, that they worried when a dog came near, that they sympathized when harm came to life near them, plant life, animal life, insect life. Some of it was pretty fantastic; Backster said that fresh vegetables "fainted" when selected to be dropped into boiling water and that even eggs, without any indication of embryonic development, "fainted" just before they were broken. A North Carolina foundation had given Backster a grant to further his research. Backster thought plants to be telepathic. He was quoted in one article: "We're getting into another dimension, a scientific twilight zone in which something can go from point to point without going between them and without consuming time to get there."

"If I hadn't seen it happen," George told Gwen, as they discussed the articles, "I'd agree with the members of the polygraph association and call him a nut."

"They feel," Gwen said.

"Something," George agreed. "Do we give up eating tomatoes?"

"I don't know. It's not quite clear."

"Maybe you knew all along," George said.

"Why do you say that?"

"Well, you've talked to the African violets and the bastards are healthier than any I've ever seen."

"Just T.L.C.," she said, trying to laugh it off.

"Think what happens when a reaper goes through a field of wheat," George said. "Thousands, millions of screams of mortal agony."

Seeing her shiver, he took her into his arms. "Look, this is all too heavy for me. I'm not going to give up greens and asparagus. I'm going to continue to keep my yard cleared. Isn't it the same as eating beef if the plants actually do feel? We know a cow feels fear and pain."

"I don't know," she said. "There is an answer, I suppose."

"Not on this earth," George said.

12

"Really, I think that it's foolish to go on spending money that way," Gwen was saying. She'd spent Monday and Tuesday in peace, the only sounds of heavy equipment coming from far across the waterway. She was clearing the breakfast table and George was finishing his second cup of coffee and frowning up at her. "He's a perfectly nice old man. He's a delightful conversationalist, but I feel as if we're paying money to have me listen to him talk, and that isn't the way it's supposed to work. Is it?"

"I have to take his machine back," George said.

"Why not wait until Friday?" she asked. "You can drop it off and we'll take in a movie or something."

"Does that mean that you're not going back to see King?"

"Do you think I need to?" She stood behind him and pressed her breasts into his shoulders. She'd taken to going braless around the house. It was nice. She was built for it and it was, for George, quite a novelty. Nothing like being able to grab a loving handful of softness unharnessed. He thought it over. She'd been a doll since the scary incident with the cat, no hang-ups, no problems.

"Well, honey, we'll leave that up to you," he said.

"I think the main thing is that by talking to Dr. King, even briefly, I've been able to talk to myself. I've learned a lot."

"Miracle cure," he said, turning to put his arms around her and pushing the side of his face into her stomach.

"Buddy, if you're planning to go to work, you'd better stop that." He was caressing the roundness of her hips.

"I really should," he said. "But I could be late."

"No," she said, laughing, pulling out of his arms. "I'll be the woman behind the man and send you off to conquer the electronics world."

"Or Sam Davis's ship-to-shore radio, as the case may be," George said, rising, kissing her and then pulling away to brush his teeth and gargle with a vigorous action. She waved him down the drive and closed the door. It wasn't that she wanted him to go. No. She wanted to be near him, always, but there were other things.

She waited for ten minutes, standing patiently just inside the door, ear cocked to catch the sound of the M.G. in case he decided to come back, in case he'd forgotten something. Then she moved quickly to the balcony overlooking the clear pond. She listened, looked, and walked down the steps, leaving her shoes on the decking. At the edge of the pond she halted and listened again. She was alone. She waded into the water, inches deep, moving her feet carefully, slipping them among the pulpy bottom growth. Ankle deep, she began to move her feet slowly, sinking them into the soft, cool sand. When they were covered, she stood very still, let her arms hang loosely at her sides, closed her eyes, and lifted her face to the sun.

At the main construction site of the generating plant there was the usual bedlam of noise, huge machines, rivet guns, welders, trucks, and voices. An official of the power company was making an inspection tour and was being given the red carpet treatment by Jack Flores, site boss for the prime contractor. The official wore a lightweight suit and a hard hat. Flores, an outside man, was in freshly pressed khaki. The tour had begun early and was being climaxed by a view of the entire site from atop the reactor building. The official was impressed. Flores was pleased, for he was four days ahead of schedule.

When the official had seen enough, they climbed down and got into a four-wheel-drive vehicle, Flores driving. He cut across the huge site, pointing out progress as he went, crossed a small highway under which the canal had been dug, a new bridge installed. Flores could see that the man was impressed. He himself always got a gut feeling when he saw a project really beginning to shape up. He'd been on some big jobs, but this one was a real gasser. He always felt as if he were back on the desert in Arizona, where he'd grown up, when he drove across the site and down the canal. The barren, roiled soil extended, a half-mile wide, on a straight line arrowing for the ocean five miles away. Man, the shit had been moved, and the trees cleared and burned. Not a blade of grass was left standing, although it would grow back eventually alongside the cooling canal.

The draglines were working, digging into the soft sand. The heat rose from them, and diesel fumes sweetened the air. Jack drove to the end of the current dig, and they were almost to the waterway. He cut off through old timber roads, made it to the beach highway, and pulled off again to give a guided tour of the vast, raw earth of the catch basin. Then he aimed the car across the bridge and onto the island. He drove quickly up to the ocean side, where work was temporarily halted on digging into the dunes. The equipment was there, untended, but then no one was going to steal a drag line mounted on a barge. He pointed out the cut where the canal would come across the island and bounced off into the raw earth toward the remaining trees.

He was a bit put out when he saw the dozer standing there idle. "Operator's taking a break, I guess," he said. He didn't really have to alibi to the power company man. The jerk didn't know from shit about construction. But when he was making a V.I.P. tour he wanted his men working, and working hard. "We're not pushing it on this end," he said. "The big job is on the other side. Then we'll be into the dredging of the marsh for a few months. There's plenty of time to finish up over here, so we've just got two machines working."

The other dozer was idle, too. Come to think of it, he hadn't seen Billy Daniels's old car down on the road. Bastards were probably laying out drunk.

From the inland edge of the last remaining trees in the area to be cleared, you could see across the marsh to the high dikes of the holding basin. Flores stopped the car and pointed out the route of the canal across the marsh. With his own clear vision, he was able to follow the line of survey flags all the way. While the power company guy was gawking, he walked to the dozer and put his hand on the side of the hood. It was cold. It hadn't even been cranked up, and it was well into the day, almost noon. Moreover, there hadn't been anything done since the last rain. He furrowed his brow. There'd been a helluva rain on Friday. That meant Daniels and Peebles hadn't hit a lick since sometime Friday, that they hadn't been in to work at all on Monday or Tuesday. He'd hand-picked them for this job and they'd let him down, but there was no real harm done. He'd been pushing construction crews long enough to know that men came and men went. Dozers could be pushed by just about any jerk with enough sense to mash pedals. He'd see to it, though, that Peebles and Daniels didn't work for any of the big boys as long as they lived. He'd put the word out on those two cruds.

He bought dinner for the visiting official in town, dropped him back at the main office, and went out onto the site. No point in trying to get anyone over on the island until the next morning. He went into his office and checked on available men, selected one, and sent him word that he wanted to see him just before the four o'clock whistle. His guess was that Daniels and Peebles would try to clock a full week's work. Judging from the progress they had made, they'd been going great guns out there. They had probably thought they'd be able to birddog it a little and take a few days off, get paid for them, and still come in with the job finished under the gun. Well, those two bastards had a surprise coming. He made a note to check their time cards on Friday, if he didn't see them before then. Meanwhile, he had a million and one things on his mind. He started on them one at a time.

The dozer started up at seven on Thursday, waking Gwen. The alarm went off a few minutes later, but she was wide awake, sitting up in bed listening. She could hear the muffled roar of the engine and could feel the results. She was preoccupied during breakfast. George asked her if she felt all right. She shook her head. "Just a little draggy," she said.

There was no peace. She stood ankle deep in wet sand, the water coming up to her calves. She swayed. The dozer clanked and growled. She wanted to scream. She wanted to move, to act. She was held back. It was too soon. There would be other opportunities for revenge, for trading death for death. Not now.

She stood in an attitude of listening, arms hanging loosely, face lifted, eyes closed. She swayed slightly. She tried to close out the pain with memories, but the magnitude of it was overpowering.

Don and Tommy Promer, brothers, aged fourteen and just under thirteen, had told all their friends about the crazy woman up on the point. "First she says, come here, then she starts screaming. A real dingaling." They'd talked about her a lot. They kept telling each other they'd go back up there and take another look. "Had her clothes almost off," Tommy, the younger, said. "We could see her boobs."

Actually, they'd seen only the tricot bra, but in memory it became bare flesh.

Both of them were large for their ages. Both were handsome, athletic, and blond. They lived an ideal life in the summer, with water everywhere, fish plentiful, a boat always ready for their use, and summer girls all over the strand. There just wasn't enough time to go hiking through the woods, being eaten by yellow flies and mosquitoes, just to see a crazy woman. But Don had sliced his foot on a broken bottle, which some jerk had thrown into the sand of the dunes down on the inlet, and he couldn't go water skiing, the fish weren't biting, and it was too early in the day to go up to the public beach to chase girls. They rode their motor bikes to the point, left them hidden in brush, walked the road almost to the house, and then cut through the brush to come out behind the pond.

She was standing next to the water, no, in the water, with a dumb look on her face. She was wearing a bikini and, wow, she was stacked. They watched for a long, long time and she didn't even move, except to sway from side to side a little bit. Tommy was spooked. "Let's get out of here," he whispered.

"In a minute." Don was taking off that bikini piece by piece. Since the pieces were small and just two in number, it wasn't much of a job. He licked his lips and let his fancy soar.

She could feel them. She opened her eyes without moving her head. She couldn't see them at first. Then she caught a glimpse of a white tee shirt through the green. She questioned. But she understood far more now. Anything, anything to ease the pain, to bring peace, even if for a limited time. She felt it rise in her, that familiar ripe, swollen feeling. She felt herself expanding, her breasts full, the blood flowing into sensitive areas.

"Hello," she called.

"She's seen us," Tommy said. "Let's move."

"Naw, she can't see us," Don, the oldest, said.

"Don't be afraid," she called.

"Who's afraid?" Tommy whispered, but he didn't move.

"Please come out," she said. "Please."

"I'm getting out of here," Tommy said.

"I'm sorry I startled you last time," she called.

Yes, yes, anything. I know. I understand.

"Come over and we'll talk," she said.

"Don't," Tommy said, trying to hold Don down. But Don stood up, and she smiled and waved at him.

"Would you like to see me without any clothes?" she called.

The boys, Tommy standing now, looked at each other.

"See?" She had dropped the bikini top. "Come closer."

"What the hell?" Don said, moving to walk around the end of the pond on the high end. Tommy followed, feeling a mixture of emotions, his eyes unable to leave the two mounds. He tumbled down, not watching where he was walking. Don stopped a few feet away.

"Do you like me?" she asked, smiling.

"You putting us on?" Don asked, his voice uncertain. He had his hand in his pocket to hide his excitement.

"No, please. Don't think that. I like you. Please come here." She held out her arms. Neither boy moved. She pushed the small bikini bottom down and let it drop. Don heard Tommy gasp behind him. "I'll do nice things for you," she said, smiling and putting one hand up to cup one of her breasts.

Don had done it with a summer girl. Tommy had never done it, although he told everyone he had. He couldn't believe it. He'd never seen a woman naked, except in pictures. The girl was moving toward them. Tommy backed off a few steps. Don stood his ground, and when she kissed him and put her hand down and squeezed his penis, he gave up, stopped thinking that it was a trap or that she was crazy.

Ripe, full, the emotions so powerful that they cut off the sound of the dozer, the pain, everything but the ripeness, the mellowness. She heard all small sounds, felt the grass under her, knew the frantic, youthful strength, urged them on, teased them, took them. "I'll show you, little darling. Like this. See? Isn't it sweet?"

And, when, inevitably, there was no more strength left to give, when the two boys were dressing sheepishly, feeling smug and tired, she said, "Please come back to see me?"

"You bet," Tommy said.

"Do you have friends?" she asked. She understood now. It was all right. Anything, anything to block off the pain, even if for a fleeting moment.

"Yeah, sure."

"Send them," she said. "Tell them to come any day but Friday, Saturday and Sunday. Will you?"

"You sure?" Don asked.

She laughed. "Well, not dozens at a time. One or two. Perhaps three."

"Some kind of nut," Don said, as they walked back toward the bikes.

"Who cares. Man, that was great."

"No one will believe us," Tommy said, after a few moments of silence.

"Who cares?" Don asked. "How many times did you go?"

"Twice," the younger boy said. "You?"

"Three times," Don said proudly. "I'll bet I can do it four next time."

13

Jack Flores was one pissed-off man. It was getting to the point where you couldn't depend on anyone. First Daniels and Peebles and now Cramer, one of his oldest, most trustworthy men. He'd decided to put just one good man on the island. Even that would have done the job in plenty of time, because the fucking environmentalists had raised a lot of new hell and had forced the chickenshit Federal people to hold up the permit on the marsh dredging until the school boys did another so-called Environmental Study of the fucking thing. That meant a thirty-day delay in starting the marsh work, and he was about ready to start moving the dredges in.

It was one thing right after the other. A couple of drunk Chicanos over on the reactor had gotten into a fight over some local whore and had gone after each other with pipe wrenches. One of them was in the hospital with a concussion and the other was in the local jail. The bastard's wife, a cute little number, was on Flores's neck, begging him to get good old Pancho out of jail. "He's a good man," she kept saying. "He's never done anything like this before. That Nogales, he started it. My Pancho was just defending himself."

"Sure, sure," Flores said. "I'll see what I can do."

"He's a good man, he has children, he goes to church."

"Sure, sure," Flores said. "Tell you what, I'll send the company lawyer over."

"Bless you, señor, you are a good man."

All that shit. He thought she was going to try to kiss his hand. He ushered her out and got on the phone to the office and gave the supervisor hell, wanting to know how much longer they were going to be held up by some fucking government red tape. And on top of that, Cramer's wife calling every hour wanting to know why Cramer hadn't come home from work on Monday. Well, hell, Flores wanted to know, too. Cramer was a good man. If he hadn't had a thing for a whiskey bottle, he'd have moved up in the company, like Flores. He didn't tell Mrs. Cramer that the bastard was probably off shacked up with some local slut, dead drunk. No. And he didn't want to do old Cramer in. The man had been with the company as long as Flores had, and when he wasn't on the bottle he was one hell of a heavy equipment man. But the sonofabitch had picked a bad time, right after Daniels and Peebles had bugged out without a word. Goddamned construction bums anyhow. Flores wished he could dig it all by hand, bring in a thousand hungry wetbacks and get the job done. To hell with construction bums.

Well, there was not much harm done. He'd given Cramer his chance. He'd put another man out there and let the bastard have his fling, but when he came back, hung over and sick, he was going to get hell. Flores would put him onto the hottest, most back-breaking piece of machinery on the job.

Late that afternoon, just ahead of the whistle, he left the job, pushed the Scout as fast as it would go, and to hell with the local fuzz, drove to the island. The new kid on the dozer there was an eager beaver. He wasn't neat and he wasted a lot of motion, but judging from his progress he'd had the Cat moving all day. He was still at it after four o'clock when Flores arrived. The kid had to be waved down.

"How'm I doing?" the kid asked, coming up to Flores.

"You ain't gonna get no prize for neatness," Flores said.

"Well, I was going to go back and clean it up after," the kid said.

"Clean it up as you go," Flores said. "And be here at seven tomorrow, O.K.?"

"Sure," the kid said.

"You drink?" Flores asked.

"I've been known to take a drink," the kid said.

"You don't drink until you've finished this job, O.K.?"

"Well, hell, Flores."

"You wanta work for me, or anyone else in this fucking business, you are a goddamned teetotaler until you knock down every mothering tree in this cut, you hear?"

"I hear," the kid said sullenly.

"You got a girl?"

"Now look," he began.

"I asked if you got a girl. You don't like my questions, there's the road."

"Well, shit. No, no one special."

"Just pick-ups, like the rest of these bums," Flores said. "Well, until you get that cut clean, you're also not interested in girls, you understand."

"You're coming on strong," the kid said, bristled up.

"I had three good men walk off this job," Flores said. "We ain't pushed, but I'm gonna see to it that we're not. We are going to put diggers on this cut in a week and you are going to have it as bald as a whore's cunt after a case of crabs in four days, you understand?"

"Sure, sure," the kid said glumly.

"You wanta pile up a little time and a half, you work on for a while. Just turn it in. Take Saturday, if you want. That is if you're interested in making a buck."

That was different. The kid grinned. "Hell, yes. Thanks, boss." He went back to the dozer and was neatening things up when Flores left.

The kid who had been ordered not to drink or chase girls obeyed part of the order. He didn't drink. He didn't care too much for it anyhow, unless it was at a party. But about the other, well, hell, when a gal comes out to the site in a set of hotpants and promises you a little if you'll go down into the woods with her, well, hell.

And while the kid was dying, (he died badly, the shot missing his throat and knocking off his lower jaw, leaving him screaming through gurgling blood, and then he wasn't dead, after the second shot, but smothered under wet sand and leaves), George was having a talk with Dr. Irving King. He'd gotten involved on the previous Friday and hadn't taken the machine back to King, but this Friday he had to go into town for supplies and he carried the polygraph in the pick-up, and delivered it to King, and then demonstrated that it was working. This led to long, involved experiments with the equipment, and he found that King was one sharp fellow and knew a lot about polygraph work. After a complete rundown on the machine and its various functions, and after they'd called in the grumbling office assistant, hooked the electrodes onto her aging carcass and played around for an hour, well into the doctor's nap time, George started telling King about his experiments with the plants. King was fascinated. He asked technical questions and examined the tapes, which George had saved. They hooked into a rubber plant which was kept alive in the outer lobby by the office assistant and got some interesting readings.

When Irving King finally lay down for his nap he was so tired he fell asleep instantly. The assistant waked him in time for his last appointment of the day and he told the woman, who was a first-timer, that what she needed was a marriage counselor, not a psychiatrist. "You keep running them away," the assistant grumbled.

"Who needs them?" King asked, putting away his papers for the day. The rubber plant was still in his office. He looked at it and mused on what George had told him and on what he, himself, had seen on the polygraph when

George crinkled one of the large leaves in his hand. Very interesting. If he were younger, he'd definitely explore it further. But he was eighty-two going on three and he was tired.

Nice kid, that George Ferrier. Smart. Fixed the damned machine so that it was working perfectly. And his wife, a nice kid, too. Too bad she had decided to drop out of treatment. She wasn't a mental basket case, but she needed help. But with a husband like George, she'd probably make it.

More interesting to speculate on those plants. Wild thought, to believe that they could receive thoughts telepathically. Opened up whole new fields of investigation. He'd have to write to Gerheart and see if he'd read anything about it.

"I'm leaving," the assistant said, sticking her head in the door. He waved impatiently. He heard the door slam and then he rose, ponderously and tiredly, stretching and feeling the weight of his body on his brittle bones. Another day. How many more? Not enough, surely. Not enough to accomplish all that he'd like to do. There was the book, for example. Every headshrinker wrote at least one, and, although he was in an area where he didn't get too many glamor cases, he'd had his share of interesting ones.

He was still thinking about the book as he drove his big car slowly toward his riverside apartment. If he had time, he would write it for popular consumption, because frankly, he didn't have the unique cases in his file to interest the profession, but he could wow the public with some of the sexual fantasies some of his patients had come up with over the years. Not exactly the height of professional ethics, but he wouldn't be the first psychiatrist to capitalize on the miseries of his patients to make a dollar. The woman who had literally split herself jamming an ivory elephant's tusk up her, rich, a member of an old family.

The young girl sent to him after taking on all of the local high school football team and then bringing herself to the attention of the authorities by yelling rape. Twenty-three boys, testifying that she'd told them it was their reward for winning the big game. Twenty-three. In sheer volume, she was the sexiest thing he'd ever run across. Then all the hang-up cases. Like Gwen. Nothing spectacular there. But, although it had never come out in his talks with her or in his chats with George, that was the reason behind it all, the woman's attitude toward sex. Natural to be hung-up a bit, with her mother putting on exhibitions the way she did. Not natural for her to drop out of analysis and live a completely happy life after only three or four visits. But George had said things were going great and he'd looked fat and sassy. No sexual frustration there, not in that boy. He literally glowed with contentment.

Speaking of books, if he were younger he could get a good one out of that plant business. Very interesting. The boy had invited him to visit and bring the machine and try it on the Venus-flytraps. He said the readings obtained there were spectacular. Might not be a bad idea, at that. A day away from the office and the apartment would do him good. Where was it they lived? Somewhere over in Ocean County. Oh, yes, on the island. Pine Tree Island. Nice name. He'd run into it before. A patient?

Damn his failing memory. He'd have Ruthie look it up next morning. No, this was Friday. He'd ask her about it Monday. She'd had plenty of time to go through the files. And there was that tantalizing something about Gwen Ferrier. She reminded him of something, and there was a nagging feeling of curiosity there, as if it were something interesting. Well, Monday, then. He'd ask her for sure, on Monday. He'd even write it down. Couldn't do it driving, although he kept a notebook in his coat pocket. Next stoplight. He'd write it down.

At the next stoplight he reached for the notebook just as a car made an illegal left turn and demolished two expensive fenders. By the time the excitement was over, he'd forgotten his notebook.

For Jack Flores, things were getting to be too much. First of all, it was hot. The early August temperature readings were setting all-time records for the state, and with the humidity, it was hell on Flores. He was used to the baking heat of the desert, where the sweat evaporated as fast as it formed. Here, it was like living in a fucking steam bath. Then you walked into the main construction office and the air conditioning hit you and dried the sweat and you shivered. He was reading the first draft of a report by the company's tame egghead, a youthful Ph.D. in Oceanography who had come in answer to an ad. Jack's immediate superior was seated across the desk, drinking a Coke and looking at Jack's furrowed brow.

"The sonofabitch is selling us out," Flores said, throwing the paper down onto the desk. "What are we paying him for, to give the nuts more ammunition against us?"

"It's not all that bad, Jack," the supervisor said.

"Bad enough." He sighed, leaned back, and lit up a Lark. "Producing marsh, shit. What does that marsh produce besides marsh grass and mud?"

"We're caught in the middle of a fad," the supervisor said. "All of a sudden people are in love with every acre of salt marsh on the eastern seaboard. But I don't think we have to worry. The new recommendations should handle all the federal boys' objections. They want a change here." He stabbed at a map of the canal route, indicating a saltwater creek. "They say we can't run right down the creek line, that would be altering the natural flow of a navigable waterway or something."

"Listen, you can't get a rowboat up that creek except on high tide. And if we move over, we're going to take that tobacco farm here." He pointed.

"Actually, we'll be better off. The engineers have come up with some new estimates," the supervisor said. He smiled. "In fact, I was the one who told our tame scientist to suggest that the creek was worth saving."

"Any particular reason?" Flores asked.

"When we move to the west, onto solid ground, we're getting an anchor for the canal. If we come down the middle of that marsh, she's going to be floating in the middle of a sea of mud. We'd have to go down thirty or fifty feet to anchor the dikes."

"Well, actually, it won't make much difference to me," Flores said. "We're not down to that point yet with the clearing. I can get the survey party out—"

"They're already out."

"Good."

"Go ahead with it, Jack. The thirty day injunction is just a nuisance, that's all. It should give you enough time to finish the clearing and get the diggers going. When we get the go ahead from the federal people, we can concentrate on the marsh."

"Right." Flores rose. He was already thinking ahead. He was halfway to the door when he was stopped.

"What's this about losing four dozer pushers over on the island?"

Flores said, "Goddamn." He turned. "Where'd you hear that?"

"Are you trying to cover up something, Jack?"

"Hell, no. I'm just trying to head something off. You know what a stupid bunch of shitheads construction bums are."

"I heard a group discussing it," the supervisor said. "I'm afraid you've got a legend going, whether you want it or not. The men are saying that something is happening to the operators over on Pine Tree Island."

"Yeah," Flores said. "They're bugging out."

"Are you sure, Jack? Four of them?"

"Hell, you don't know these bums like I do. Cramer will probably be back. When he really goes on one, he's good for two weeks and then he's so fucking messed up he can't work for another week. The first two were just drifters." He sighed. He didn't mention the kid. That one he couldn't figure. The kid had had an opportunity to pick up a good, solid piece of extra cash with overtime, and he'd looked damned interested. Then he'd bugged out, after working late Friday and all day Saturday, without even turning in the time.

"What are you going to do about it?" the supervisor asked.

"Put two men on the machines tomorrow morning. We're not pushed over there."

"Do you think it would be a good idea to send a guard along?"

"Hell, no."

"The men—"

"The men do what I tell them to do," Flores said. "They know the country's full of construction bums."

"Jack, we're in the red on this project as far as accidents are concerned."

"Fights, stupidity."

"I don't think a man falling into the reactor hole was the result of a fight," the supervisor said. "And it was stupid of that fellow to get under a fresh load of cement, all right, but the fact is, we've had too many fatalities already. This company has always been proud of its safety record. We're able to get men with that record and I don't want it ruined. And I didn't like the way those men were talking about the four fellows who have disappeared from the Pine Tree clearing area. I think I'd feel better if you sent along a guard."

"And admit that we think something might be fucked up over there?"

"What if we lose another man or two?"

Flores shrugged. "You're the boss."

"Not out on the site," the supervisor said. "But if you like, you can say that I wanted the guard."

"I could just tell them to work within sight of each other."

"Do that. And tell the guard to stay close to both of them."

Flores gave in. He was already wet with sweat by the time he drove back to the work shack and checked his boards. He made his choice, sent his notices, called security, and told them to detail a man to the Pine Tree site at seven o'clock. Then he said fuck all and drove over to check out the newly surveyed route for the canal cut.

14

Tommy Promer, aged thirteen, held front stage center. He'd kept his secret as long as it was possible, because Don had told him that they had a good thing going and there was no sense messing it up, even if she did keep asking them to send or bring friends.

You can only listen to guys brag for so long without opening up to tell them that even if some of them are older, they don't know beans about it.

Don was off with a girl. Tommy had ridden his motor bike to the Leaning Pine Fishing Pier. The August night was perfect for sitting out on the end of the pier, in the glow of light from the last lamp post, listening to the ocean moving restlessly underneath, washing the barnacle-studded steel pilings as it pushed low swells toward the strand. Tommy liked to watch the waves from the backside. He spent a lot of hours on the pier, day and night, watching the waves and figuring them out so that the next time he was down there with his surfboard he could know which one to take and which ones to let ride under him. At night the waves looked sort of spooky. The lights of the pier glowed on them and made them look bigger than they were and they'd disappear into the darkness between lamp posts and reappear and then, near the strand, they would hump up and get steep on the front and then fall into the white of surf.

A couple of the guys were out there shark-fishing when Tommy walked out, a Coke in his hand. He lay down on a fishy-smelling bench and watched. One of the guys hooked into a two-footer, a small one. Tommy leaned over the railing and watched, finished his Coke, tossed the cup into the sea, and offered comments as the shark ran and pulled the drag on the reel. It was a lazy, fine night and the talk, after the shark had been pulled up, stabbed repeatedly, thrown back, was idle.

Couples, mostly island guys and summer girls, would walk out, say hi, stand around watching the lack of action, and then walk away. Guys began to drift out as the evening progressed. They'd made the rounds, failed to make a pick-up or weren't interested, and the little group at the end of the pier gradually grew until there were eight boys ranging in age from Tommy's thirteen to about eighteen. One of them started bragging about a summer girl he'd just been out with. According to the way he told it he was the world's best lover and the girl had practically raped him. Tommy snorted. After three trips up to the point, he felt that he was a man of experience.

Once started, the talk, naturally, stayed on the subject of girls and, in particular, what girls carried in their pants and how best to get to it. Everyone, Tommy discovered, was an authority. One guy of about sixteen was telling how, once he'd done it, this summer girl played with his cock until it got hard again. Tommy said, "There's a better way."

They laughed. Being the youngest, Tommy came in for a lot of kidding. "What do you know about it?" the last bragger asked.

"If she really wants to get it up fast," Tommy said, "she gives you a blow job."

There was laughter and general comment, the gist of which was that Tommy would go like a skyrocket if a girl even looked at his cock.

About that time Cowboy Gore came ambling out. Cowboy was an old guy, but he was nutty. His hair was gray and long and he smoked all the time, so that his fingers were always brown with nicotine stains. He smelled like he hadn't had a bath in a year or so. Cowboy was always hanging around. He had a trust fund set up and some lawyer in town doled out a few bucks a month to keep Cowboy in cigarettes and pay his meal ticket at the little restaurant on the old boat basin. Cowboy had just enough sense to know that he could afford just about one six-pack of beer a week if he wanted to keep himself in smokes. He spent a lot of time walking the roads to the beach, picking up bottles and cashing them in for the two-cent deposit. He'd save his pennies until he had enough for a six-pack, and then the six-pack would make him roaring drunk. He always wore a pair of boots and a hat, and that's why they called him Cowboy. He was sort of a town clown, and the younger boys found him useful sometimes, for the merchants all knew him and would sell him beer. He'd go in and buy a six-pack for you if you gave him one. He was always hanging around and they didn't mind, because he just listened, most of the time. His mind was so weak that he couldn't follow most of the talk. He leaned on the railing and smoked, drawing on the cigarette with wide, Hollywoodish gestures.

"You ever had a blow job?" Tommy asked the loudest laugher.

"One thing for sure, you haven't," the older boy said.

"Wanta bet?" His very smugness made him sound truthful. For once, they listened. And he, being front stage center for once, told them all of it. He told it so convincingly that there was silence until he was finished and then some quiet laughter. The laughter was subdued, because Tommy had told it so well there was a sticky, musky feeling in the air.

"You've been reading dirty books," said one of the older boys. There was, however, no conviction in his voice. There'd been a ring of truth in Tommy's story.

"He's right," Cowboy said. It was so rare for Cowboy to talk that they all looked at him. "He's right."

"You tell 'em, stud," someone said, trying for a laugh.

"You just go up and you whistle," Cowboy said.

There was a chorus of catcalls and laughter. Cowboy looked disturbed. He worked his lips, trying to find words.

"Boy, if she'd take on old Cowboy I don't want any of that," someone said.

"She's—pretty," Cowboy said.

"Shut up, Cowboy," Tommy said, his stature fading faster than it had been built.

"And she likes—" He couldn't find the word. He made a circle of his fingers and punched his forefinger into it, grinning at them.

"He's gonna beat your time," someone called out to Tommy.

"You're lying, you dumb bastard," Tommy yelled at Cowboy. "You don't even know who I'm talking about."

"Girl—up there," Cowboy said, pointing toward

the north end of the island, the point. "Very pretty." He punched his finger into the ring of his thumb and forefinger and smirked. "Big house. You whistle."

"Now wait a minute," one of the older guys said. "Are you saying you've screwed this broad, Cowboy?"

"Long time," Cowboy said. "Long time."

"When, you bastard?" Tommy said, standing in front of Cowboy and looking up into his wizened face. "This week? Last week? Last month?"

"Long, long time," Cowboy said, wrinkling his forehead in thought and making theatrical gestures with his cigarette.

"This year?" Tommy asked.

"Long time."

"Has it been winter since you screwed her?" Tommy asked. "Was it this summer or has it been cold since you screwed her?"

"Cold, lots of times," Cowboy said.

"This girl has only lived there since the winter," Tommy said.

"Looks like you and Cowboy both got great imaginations," someone said.

"Look, damnit, I'll prove it to you. She's been asking us to bring a friend. One of you bastards think you're man enough to take on a real woman, you can come along."

"Whoooo," they yelled. Tommy tried to yell them down, but he was outnumbered and then the conversation failed as another shark snared itself on one of the rigs and Tommy went off alone, still smug in his knowledge that there was a girl up there and thinking that he was going up there on Monday and a little pissed-off because no one would believe him.

Mack Allen followed him into the pier house and sat beside him on a stool at the counter. Tommy had another Coke. Mack said, after a long time, "You're not lying?"

"Up you," Tommy said angrily. Mack sat silently for a long time.

"Want me to go with you?"

Tommy snorted. "I ain't begging. Me and Don can handle it."

"How about I go with you next time?"

"Suit yourself," Tommy said. "I'm going Monday morning."

"Yeah, O.K.," Mack said. "I'll come on over to your house early. O.K.?"

"Suit yourself," Tommy said, wondering what Don was going to say.

For a few days the guard on the Pine Tree cut was alert. He walked around in his uniform, his gun at his side, and watched the big Cats tear into the trees with roaring efficiency. After a few days, however, it became apparent to the guard that those other guys had just taken off. Construction workers were like that. There was a big operation getting underway down in South America and he wouldn't have been surprised to know that at least a couple of the four missing guys had just decided to go south. There certainly was no threat apparent on the island. The woods looked sort of thick, but they contained nothing more than a few foxes and a coon, maybe. There were no houses around, not within a half mile to the north and about the same on the south, with a new golf course coming right up to the edge of the cut on the south side. About the only danger the guard could see was the danger of being hit in the head with a stray golf ball if you went over on the south side of the cut near one of the few places where you could see through to the course. So after a while he found himself a shady spot where he could sit and watch both Cats working, unless one of them went around on the other side of the diminishing bunch of trees in the cut. He didn't see it happen.

One of the bulldozers was pushing fallen trees into a pile. The pile was a huge one. The higher you made it the better it would burn when the burners came around, after a few days of drying out. The operator had his blade low and was digging in in the lowest gear to push the pile into a more compact mass. It was an accident, a freak thing that should never have happened. In the mass of broken trees in front of the dozer there was a young pine, about five inches thick at the base. It had been pushed out easily, its tap root broken just below the ground. Its branches had been stripped by rolling and crushing in the mass of trees. But it was lying near the top now, full length, its small end pointed toward the dozer. The tip had been broken, too, leaving a jagged point about two inches in thickness. The jagged end was lodged against a small oak limb and the butt end was pushed solidly against a large pine. The pressure bent it, compressed it into a bow. Just as the Cat began to bog down, unable to compress the mass further, the jagged end snapped free of the oak and the compression of the flexible young tree was released suddenly, sending it lancelike and deadly, under the protective cage on the machine and to pierce the operator just in the vee of his rib cage. No one heard his scream. The young pine went through, severing the backbone, punching a hole in the leatherette upholstery of the seatback. The big Cat spun its treads, slewed off, blade ripping free of the mass of trees. The guard saw it lumbering across the clearing toward the northern tree line, rose to see what was going on. The pine, embedded in the operator's body, was extending out over the hood, heavy end bouncing up and down as the Cat rocked over the rough ground. The guard gave chase, but he knew nothing about heavy equipment. The Cat hit the tree line, crashed through and over small brush, and thudded into a huge oak, where it stopped, spun tracks, and then choked down.

It was clearly an accident, but Flores had four straight operators tell him, hell, no, they weren't going over there. That was a jinx job.

Now there were too many of them. Two men on the machines, a guard, and others coming around during the day. All she could do was stand back in the woods, out of sight, and watch. Now the other was even more important. Now it was vital to her to have the visitors, for only then could she close her mind to the rending pain. The first two were still her favorites, but she liked the others, too. And there were always new ones coming. Usually she waited for them, standing in the clean, cool water, the soothing sand over her feet, the brushing touch of the plants on her legs. But sometimes they'd come when she was inside, and then they would stand by the pond and whistle until she went out. Then she'd feel ripe, swollen, and at peace. Then she'd blank out the noise of the bulldozers and the pain and afterwards she'd be rewarded with memories, with the delightful feeling of eternal peace and love and immortality.

Some of them wanted to swim in the pond afterwards. She'd let them, telling them to be very careful. Once two of them started a water fight in the shallows and, in their enthusiasm, ripped plants from the sand. She told them not to come back.

By mid-August the Pine Tree Island cut was complete. Black smoke swelled into the humid air. Workers carried large cans of waste oil and other inflammables to help ignite the piles of broken trees. The fires burned for days, were put out by heavy rains, reignited. When it was finished, two bulldozers smoothed the ravaged area, leaving white sand, spotted here and there with torn, red, broken roots.

The pain was over, but it had been so vast, so extended,

that her nerves were raw, tingling. She ached with the memory of it, dreamed it was back, thought with fierce satisfaction of the four decomposing bodies hidden in her woods, covered with dirt and sand and leaves, filling the empty sockets, of trees blown down, in past storms, returning something to the earth which they had torn and ravaged.

There were still sounds, but now it was the sounds made by the diggers and earth movers and that was bearable. Inside, with the air conditioner running, she could scarcely hear them. One by one, she told the visitors not to return. Some of them were not convinced, came to stand beside the pond, whistling, until, she supposed, their whistlers got tired and they went away. The danger of one of them coming kept her from the pond. Now it was only in the early morning, with the sun red and the heat of the day still ahead, that she could stand, feet wet, buried in sand, and feel the peace. Soon, however, only the youngest came. She, in pity, called him inside, padded nakedly ahead of him to the living room couch, gave him pleasure.

"You're very sweet," she said, "but you mustn't come again."

"Why?"

"If you come again, I'll scream and tell my husband," she said, wanting it ended.

Well, Tommy thought, walking slowly away toward his hidden bike, now he knew how. And there were still a lot of summer girls down along the strand.

15

The editor of the *Ocean City Weekly* was a fourth generation native of the area. Back in the days when land had been priced at fifty cents an acre, and large plots had often been sold for back taxes, one of his forebears had built large holdings which had remained largely intact down through the years, mainly because no one wanted to pay good money for bays, sand-hill pines, and scrubby oak. The good timber had long since been sold off. Aside from a few twisted trees unsuited for lumber, the largest longleaf pine in the county wouldn't have made three good two-by-fours. Fast-growing loblolly pine had replaced the longleaf, and about every twenty years a landowner could sell enough loblolly for pulpwood to pay a few years' taxes. For decades, Ocean County was a depressed area. But there was the river, a large one in its lower stages, with enough water to take the untreated sewage of Port City, absorb the mercury and other wastes of the upstream industries, and still be liquid enough to be suitable for cooling large atomic reactors. The editor had politicked openly for the power plant, and not solely because he owned a few hundred acres of land unsuited for much save industry. He had a true interest in the people of the county, and was of the opinion that industry was the one hope. He worked with the newly hired industrial consultant, whose salary was paid with county funds, to bring the power company officials down for oyster roasts and tours of the county.

Never had there been, in modern times, a place more open to development. Land values were low. There was a surplus labor supply, as witness the crowds at the courthouse every week on unemployment-check day. Of course, a large influx of people would strain the antiquated school system severely, but the property taxes paid by industry would build new schools.

Just incidentally, the editor sold five hundred acres of riverside bays and sand for a price which set a new record in the county. Just incidentally, he owned a plot of the most beautiful residential development land on the lower river, just outside of town. Taxes cut into his profit, but by taking the long term capital gain he still was able to hold onto a respectable chunk of cash. The houses were going up three and four at a time in his housing development and doing well, selling almost as fast as they were laid out.

The prime contractor of the nuclear generating plant brought in a couple of thousand outside workers and their families and took off the slack in the local labor market. Bills were being paid for the first time by people who had, in the past, depended on fishing for their income. Merchants were building new buildings to handle the increase. When the job let off a shift at four in the afternoon, it was a thirty minute stop-and-go drive from Main Street to the edge of town. The local law enforcement agencies were worked to the breaking point, but that was a price to be paid for progress. The editor's circulation had jumped by several hundred, and he knew the source of the increase. As a result, he had at least one story a week about the new plant and did his best to mention as many names as possible, concentrating on the supervisors and power company people. Meanwhile, he was talking to the representatives of a large chemical company about an industrial site of four hundred acres adjacent to the raw cut in the landscape made by the power plant. The price per acre was roughly equivalent to the cost of producing Florida citrus land.

The weekly's new prosperity made it possible to hire a new reporter-photographer. He came into the office with an eight-by-ten blow-up of the dozer operator with a ten-foot length of pine sapling protruding from his belly. The editor found the picture to be interesting and well done, but a little gory for a family audience. The reporter sent the picture off to a national sensational tabloid, along with a story. The story ran in the national tabloid and, in a one paragraph squib on the inside pages, in the *Ocean City Weekly*. The freak nature of the accident appealed to the rewrite man on the City Desk at the Port City daily, and it was in the morning Port City News that Dr. Irving King read about the accident. The dateline, Pine Tree Island, reminded him that he had not, as yet, satisfied his curiosity about what it was that reminded him of something regarding his recent patient, Gwen Ferrier. The account of the death triggered other long-hidden memories.

It was a slow day in the office. The doctor went to the files and started rummaging around in the years from 1935 on. Ruthie, out for coffee, surprised him and reprimanded him for messing up her files.

"If you'd do what I asked you to," he said grumpily, "I wouldn't have to mess around in your precious files."

"If you'd tell me what it is you want," she retorted, equally grumpily, "I'd get it."

"Something to do with plants," he said.

"That tells me a lot," Ruthie said. "Flowers?"

"Plants in general. Trees, grass, weeds, all of it."

"I don't recall ever having a plant as a patient," the assistant said.

"The patient was human, and, I think, female."

"You're a gold mine of information," Ruthie said. "All right, I have nothing better to do." She said it with evident suffering, the overworked female. "So I'll spend my morning looking through the files for a female patient who had a love affair with plants."

"Do that," King said, going into his office to meditate on the perversity of all women.

He had an appointment with a young man who feared that he had homosexual tendencies. They were well into it, this being the latest in a long series going back some four months. By this time King was positive that the lad not only had tendencies, but was a flaming closet queen, and King was tempted to tell him to forget fighting it and just enjoy it. One way, he was thinking, as the young man talked endlessly about his mother's fondness for his younger sister. King covered a yawn and murmured, "Yes, go on, please."

Then he began to wonder why he did it. Why did he keep the office open? He didn't need the money, and he'd long since given up hope of getting a really interesting patient. Most of it was so damned repetitive. He would have loved to get his teeth into someone like the Boston Strangler. Now there was a psycho.

"Ruthie," he said, when the potential queen had minced out, "why don't we take down the shingle?"

"Coming to this office every day is the only thing that keeps you alive," she said bluntly. "You wouldn't last a month in retirement."

"I don't know," he said. "It seems so futile sometimes."

"Feeling sorry for ourself today, is that it?"

"I don't need the money," King said. "Not that I'm so damned rich, it's just that I won't live long enough to spend what I have."

"I don't share your fortunate estate," Ruthie said. "And I don't think I could walk down the street and get another job." She was holding a yellowed folder in her hand.

"There's enough for both of us," King said.

"Halvers?" She smiled.

"Why not?" He was remembering her at forty, a long-legged, mature woman with a Rubens body, soft and full of delights. "Are you so old and set in your ways that you couldn't adjust to living with me?"

There was a softening in the old, wrinkled face. "I've been putting up with you for thirty-five years, Irving King."

"Yes."

"You're just tired. Forget your laxative?"

"Ah, the practical mind of the woman," he said, folding his hands in front of him. "You think, to put it bluntly, that I'm just full of shit."

"That may be," she said, still smiling. He was looking at her with his face formed in a musing expression. "Let's see how you feel about it tomorrow?"

"I was just thinking," he said. "You mentioned once that you wanted to go to Greece. Did you ever make it?"

"On a two weeks' vacation?" She snorted.

"We could go," he said. "Would you like that?"

She sat on the edge of his desk and touched his shoulder. "Irving King, you're an old war horse. This office has been your life for too long. And I'm the same way. Sometimes I think how nice it would be, when the alarm goes off, to just throw it out the window and turn over and go back to sleep. But on Saturday and Sunday, when I could sleep late, I'm wide awake at seven, as usual. By Sunday evening, I'm going stir-crazy. The apartment is too small. There's no smell of cigars and there's nothing to do. By Monday morning I feel as if I'm starting a new life when I get on the bus and head downtown. Now just what would we do in retirement? Play checkers?"

"Go to Greece?"

"And have to hire strong Greek boys to carry us up the steps of the Parthenon?" She patted him on the shoulder. "Get to work, old man. It's all we have."

"There's a new condominium going up on the river," King said. "I've got a dollar invested in it. There's a unit on the first floor—" He cleared his throat and reached for a cigar. "I'd guarantee the smell of good Havana."

"All right," she said simply.

"Fine," he said.

"I think this is what you want," she said, standing, all business again. "A Mrs. Evelyn Rogers."

How in the hell could he have forgotten that one? He reached for the folder eagerly, not even noticing that Ruthie had smiled at him and shaken her head fondly before leaving. His mind was worse than he thought, to forget that one. His own Boston Strangler, his own Winnie Ruth Judd. Only it had never been proven.

If he ever did a book, she'd be in it. She just might be the prime attraction. He opened the folder. Cute address: Cutesy, more the word. Mrs. Evelyn Rogers, The Jolly Rogers, Pine Tree Island.

She had been brought to him by her husband, a man considerably older than she, on July 10, 1937. He had caught her fornicating with a local retarded teenager. His investigation had showed only rampant nymphomania, and, later, took on more interesting aspects.

As he read, his memory came back, clear, vivid. She was not a beautiful woman, but she was youthful, twenty-nine and in her prime. She talked openly about her affairs, and their variety had, he remembered with a wry smile, had the effect of good pornography on his libido. Only his professional detachment had kept him from doing something foolish. That and a truly shocked sorrow at the waste of a life. She had children, two boys and a girl, ranging in age from ten to three years. The oldest, a girl, knew what was happening, although she was often told to play in her bedroom with the younger children and not come out on pain of severe punishment. But she was a totally sexual being, and she spoke of her activities not with shame, but with a sort of detachment, as if some other woman had been involved, not she.

"They come when they know that he is away," he read. The typescript was faded, and he had to remove his glasses and hold the page close to his face. "If I'm not outside, they whistle. Then I know and I go out."

"Why, do you suppose?" he'd asked.

"It stops the pain."

"What pain?"

His interest had been given another jolt by her answer. He'd condensed it in his notes, and it had been transcribed from his rapid scrawl by the efficient Miss Ruth Henley. It had to do, he had gathered, although she was not perfectly clear, with a logging operation. The timber on Pine Tree Point, in 1937, was not virgin, but it was old stands, untouched for a hundred years. She had talked about the constant round of saws and axes, the rumblings of the logging trucks, and the vulgar talk of the loggers. And she'd talked about the trees, how they hurt when the ax bit in, and how it made her want to scream.

It had not all come out in one session. It had been scattered through weeks of treatment, but then it had begun to make a picture and now, as he read, it began to take shape.

She had asked her husband, begged her husband to cease the timbering. But 1937 was a hard year, and, apparently, Paul Rogers desperately needed money. She mentioned the cost of the large house. She said once that Paul was worried about money, something about his northern investments going bad.

"Tell him, Dr. King. Tell him it's his fault. Tell him I only do it because it hurts. Tell him I'll stop if he'll stop the pain."

The file was relatively thin. The series of treatments had been terminated abruptly. It was closed out by a newspaper story about the tragic death of Mr. and Mrs. Paul Rogers in a flash fire at their luxurious home on Pine Tree Island. All the bodies except Evelyn's had been discovered in their beds, or what was left of the bodies and the beds. Human bodies are devilishly difficult to burn, and there was enough left for identification purposes. Rogers's remains were discovered in the area of the master bedroom. The three children had died in their own beds. Evelyn Rogers, horribly burned, did manage to get out of the house. She was found several hundred yards from the house, with her body half-submerged in the waters of a small, natural pond. Her clothing had been burned off. Sheer speculation by the newspaper writer had her running from the house in flames. The fire had spread to the thick brush around the house. Perhaps, it was speculated, she ran ahead of the flames, seeing relief for her terrible pain in the water.

End. Finish. But then, a young psychiatrist had seen more than was stated in the newspaper article. In fact, King, knowing the degree of disturbance in his patient, had called the Ocean County Coroner. There were notes regarding the content of his conversation with the political hack who held the office, along with marginal notations of his dissatisfaction with the information received. No, the coroner had not performed autopsy on the remains; there were not enough remains to work with. No, the coroner was not a medical doctor. No, there were no facilities in Ocean County to make the kind of detailed analysis which Dr. King requested. Waste of time, anyhow. It was evident what had happened.

End of case.

Except for three more clippings, also dated in 1937, late in the year. A decomposing corpse had been discovered by loggers working on Pine Tree Island. The remains were identified as being those of one J. Edgar Smith, Negro, a former employee of the sawmill operator doing the logging. A protracted search of the area turned up three other bodies, also black, also former employees of the sawmill operator. In the South, in 1937, if a Negro had been turned in as missing by his relatives to the local law enforcement officers, the officers would have laughed. Everyone knew the shiftlessness of Negroes. Three dead Negroes, more or less, even four, made only inside pages of the newspapers.

Yes, King thought, putting the file back in its folder, he'd had his chance, and he'd blown it. There was, of course, no direct evidence; but Evelyn Rogers had been one disturbed young lady. A woman, young, strong, healthy, who shared the pain of trees as they were cut was not exactly normal. His notes indicated a huge reservoir of latent hostility toward her husband, whom she blamed for the logging. Most mass murderers had some sexual problem, and Evelyn Rogers had hers. It was entirely within the realm of possibility that the deaths of the Rogers family had not been accidental. Paul Rogers knew of his wife's infidelity. In his one talk with Rogers, King had seen a man embittered, a man full of anger. He'd talked freely, with great emphasis on the fact that his wife's lover was a retarded boy, big for his size but with the mentality of a six-year-old. And there was the matter of the dead loggers. Four strong Negro men. But give a woman the proper weapon and she can be deadly, even against strong men.

Too bad. If she had lived, he would have offered his services. He'd have worked for nothing, just to have the chance to pry into such a mind.

But that was in the past and now his curiosity was satisfied. To himself, for the first time, he admitted that he had neither the time nor the energy to write his book, that it would never be written. Evelyn Rogers, interesting as she was, would die, once again, when he died. His will provided that his files be destroyed.

Too bad. If he had known all, if he'd had a chance to talk with the woman, he might have been able to—to what? Satisfy his craving for sensation? Please his ego with an article about an interesting aberration? Help? Save lives?

Perhaps it was time to quit. Wasn't his attitude toward the potential homosexual a clear sign that he was no longer interested in the welfare of his patients? Once he could have become totally involved in the case, worried about it and thought of ways to help. When the patient no longer seemed important, then it was time to take down his shingle.

He chewed on the cigar, which had long since gone out. No use fighting it. Nature herself would solve the problem soon enough. Meanwhile, as Ruthie had said, what else was there? Greece? He'd have to carry an extra steamer trunk just to contain enough medication to last the both of them. One reason why he'd never married was a recognized desire to retain all his freedoms, and now he was tied to his medicine cabinet even more securely than he would have been tied to a family. He could have married. Ruthie, at thirty, was a real woman. Then he'd not had the time. Had prized his freedom.

He tossed the closed file folder onto the front of his desk. That was a part of his past and, unearthed, it lost something. At least, before Ruth dug it out, there was a little hint of curiosity, something to occupy his mind now and then when he thought about it. Having read it, he saw no real connection with anything. True, both Evelyn Rogers and Gwen Ferrier had sexual problems, but they seemed to be diametrically opposed. From what he'd gathered, Mrs. Ferrier's problem was sexual repression, not an overly free expression of sexual desire. What was it that had led his subconscious mind to make a connection between the two cases? Probably just the coincidence of residence. Pine Tree Island was a remote, thinly populated area. It was remarkable enough that he'd have two patients, even years apart, from the Island. That was probably it. Perhaps a bit of the plant business, too. For he'd gathered from the Ferriers that they had some interest in plants. George had remarked on the health of the fly-traps transplanted inside by his wife, and he had laughingly said that they were happy because his wife talked to them and pampered them with food. But Gwen Ferrier wasn't identifying with plants, as had Evelyn Rogers, and Gwen Ferrier had not done in a family and possibly four plant killers.

"The diner has fried eggplant on the menu," Ruth said, poking her head in the door.

"Fine," he said. He took her arm. "Shall we lunch in elegance and grace at the famous greasy spoon of Port City?"

"Don't forget your antacid tablets," Ruth said.

16

Work on the cross-marsh canal began in mid-August. On low tide, vehicles with huge, wide rubber tires marked the late summer greenness, pushing swatches of marsh grass down into the underlying black mud. Lumbering, tall, awkward-looking drag lines mounted on barges began to dig. The line of the canal avoided the open water, since the engineers preferred to anchor the canal to the most solid of the marsh areas. Thus the forward progress of the diggers and the big-wheeled vehicles took a three-hundred-yard bite out of the healthiest of the tall, swaying grass.

Once George had jokingly remarked that assuming that plants felt pain, what mass agony would ensue when a reaper crossed a wheat field. Actually, she knew, he was not altogether wrong. When ripe wheat is harvested, the old, brown stalk are almost vacated. The life force has been concentrated in the seeds. Thus, the mutilation of the stalks is almost painless and the wheat seeds are tough and hardly feel the operation. Of course, there is some pain, for some seeds are crushed. But the real tragedy of a wheat field comes when the seeds, the harvested wheat, are utilized.

She understood all of it now. Since the clearing operation had been completed, bringing a temporary lull in the mass pain, she'd had time to stand in the edge of the shallow water and communicate. She was more and more a part of it. She was able to submerge herself in it and know the true peace. But when the canal digging began she screamed aloud, the sound piercing the unpeopled woodlands and startling birds and a curious squirrel.

She watched them from the island. They were far across the marsh. There was no way to reach them and inflict pain in return. There was only suffering. And suffering could be momentarily eased in only one way. She drove down the island to the pier, saw some of her former friends, and issued invitations: It began again and, her soul hungering for the release, bloomed quickly into what ordinary people would have considered a bull market in promiscuity. However, she was no ordinary person. To her had been revealed a Utopia, a heaven of coexistence. That communication was mostly one-way was a problem. She could not explain. And, unable to explain, she soon lost the conviction of her own knowledge and shared the incomprehension. It was incredible that such pain could be doled out in such mass quantities. Yet it continued. In the healthy marsh, where the black mud was covered at high tide and kept eternally wet, the grass grew to a thickness of about ten individuals per square inch. One bite of a drag line killed a square yard or more. And with the grass, numbering quickly into the millions, went thousands of snails and periwinkles. Gleaming white angel wings were ripped from the deep mud, along with razor clams, quahogs, oysters near the edges of the small, watery runs, other varieties.

Truly it was the Planet of Death.

In many ways it was worse than the clearing of the trees, for there death had been an incisive blade or a massive rending. Here it often was a slow, lingering death, smothered, crushed under tons of mud, jostling along in the carriers to the spill area, interment under one's fellows and an absence of sun, and air. Death did not cease to hurt suddenly, but ached like a sore tooth and the multiplication of death was enough to disturb the very air, itself, make it heavy with sorrow, rancid with decaying vegetation, acrid with soundless screams. And she felt it all and tried, encouraging the ripe, swollen feeling, to drown it permanently in flesh. But eager as they were, those young boys and young men who came often to the point, numerous as they were, it was impossible to fill twenty-four hours with the anesthesia of carnality. And as the digging approached the island, the screams grew louder.

George was concerned. He couldn't put his finger on it, but there was something wrong. She was dreaming again, not sleeping well. Many times he'd awake, missing the soft heat of her in his bed, and find her walking the room, or staring out the window, or merely sitting wide awake in a bedroom chair, her cigarette glowing in the dark. It was not the same old problem, he knew that. Never again would he be concerned with his wife's lack of sensuality. In fact, the change in that respect was gratifyingly spectacular. He teased her about having to call in outside help, but he bore up manfully under her demands and, in fact, loved it.

But there were dark shadows under her eyes. She was not eating properly. She was losing weight. Her waist was flat and thin and her breasts were smaller, but tighter. She was, he told her often, one sexy-looking broad, but why didn't she go to a doctor or something and find out why she wasn't sleeping? He bought non-prescription sleep aids and forced them on her. Then he called Doc Braws and got, without an office call, a mild sleeping pill which worked equally as ineffectively as the non-prescription drugs.

His life, on the whole, was a dreamy, pleasant one. Semi-retired, working only because he enjoyed it, owning his own large acres, a nice house, and a private swimming pond which he used often, a beautiful, sexy wife who was his friend as well as his lover, he had no complaints, save for his worry about her health. However, she continued to paint a bit, kept the house clean and orderly, and cooked great meals with an emphasis on the things George liked, meats and seafoods. If he noticed the lack of fresh vegetables on the table he pretended not to, because he wasn't fond of fresh vegetables anyhow. There were always enough canned foods in the house to provide a balance, and he took his morning vitamin pill without fail.

They managed to extract only one life in return. It was a happy accident, at that. Jack Flores, pleased with the progress of the canal-marsh crossing, was looking over the site. He borrowed a marsh buggy, a vehicle without a top which almost floated on high, wide rubber wheels, and drove the length of the surveyed route. The dredges had moved in behind him, following in the wake of the drag lines which were stripping the vegetation and top mud away, getting down to pulpy stuff which could be sucked up and pumped away through the long dredge pipes extending across the waterway to the two-mile-long spill basin. He had crossed the waterway in a small plastic boat and had noted that the operation was muddying the waters, but a vast amount of tidal flow swept down the waterway and would, according to his engineers, carry the silt away without silting up the waterway itself to a great degree. If it did, well, he had the dredges to dig it out again. He watched the operation for a while and chuckled as a group of small boys in boats yelped and played as they, too, watched man alter nature. Then he got into the marsh buggy and drove out toward the island into marsh which hadn't yet been spoiled by the digging. There were tracks to follow. It was tricky driving a marsh buggy, because the marsh was cut by numerous guts, and near the guts the mud was bottomless. It wouldn't look good for the boss to get a buggy stuck and have to call for help, so he was careful to stay on solid ground.

The little vehicle chugged along at a smooth pace and flushed out what the locals called marsh hens, long-legged black birds of the rail family which flew awkwardly. When a marsh hen came up, its stubby wings beat against the tips of the grass for long moments before it freed itself to struggle a few yards downwind. Flores had hunted the erratic, wild Mexican quail of the Southwest, and he disdained the slow, awkward flight of the hens, wondering how anyone could find sport in shooting anything so easy to hit. But it was sort of funny the way they squawked as they were flushed out, wings fighting the air, long necks outthrust.

He was nearing the sandy cut on the island, with only a few yards of marsh between him and solid ground. He was feeling good. The job was on schedule, all the problems had not been solved, but were at least under control. He could almost see in his mind the print in his contract which guaranteed him one hell of a bonus when he brought the canal in on time. Then a big marsh hen came up right under his wheels and for a moment, Flores was a kid. He jerked the wheel of the buggy and followed the bird, the hood of the vehicle almost touching its long legs. He held no malice toward the terrified bird. It was only a game. He was just horsing around. There was good solid marsh under the wheels, and he juiced the vehicle as the bird started to draw away, steering to stay with it. "Fly, you mother," he yelled gleefully, pleased with the bird, which was staying in the air much longer than they usually did. He was so intent on staying with the bird that he didn't notice the change in color to a deeper green, which indicated that there was a small gut ahead in the grass. The vehicle's front wheels hit, sank, stopped the forward motion. The gut was a tiny one, so narrow that the grass almost closed over the top of it. Flores flew through the air. He hadn't bothered to strap himself in. The gut was a curving, snaky one and he flew over a bend and landed in a foot of water on living oysters. The shells dug in, cut, ripped. He landed with one arm under him, and he heard it snap. He lay there, dazed, the pain held back by the initial shock. He was just a few yards from the solid earth of the island. He looked down and saw that he was cut. He couldn't tell how badly, but his blood was staining the water which lay, black and muddy, in the bottom of the gut.

He tried to move and his arm hurt. He felt weak. He had cut his head, too, and the blood was flowing down into his eyes. He tried to wipe it away, but his hands were muddy. He went dizzy and lay still. When he could see again, he washed his hands in the muddy water and then tried to clear his eyes. He wondered if his accident had been observed, but he doubted it. The work force was all the way over on the other side of the marsh.

He crawled a few feet, finding it easy to make his way through the mud and water as long as he lay flat. He was so weak he began to worry a little. He figured he might have a slight concussion. Then he heard someone coming through the marsh, feet sucking and slapping the wet mud. "Hey," he called.

He looked up through mud and blood and saw a woman. She was standing on the more solid mud, looking down on him as he lay in the bottom of the small gut. "Hey, get a couple of the men," he said, surprised to hear himself sounding as if he were half dead, his voice weak and puny. "I think I've got a broken arm."

"Are you with them?" she asked, not moving her head, staring at him.

"Huh?"

"Are you with the people who are killing the marsh?"

"Oh, yeah. Listen, honey." He tried to sit up and couldn't make it. "Listen, I'm hurting. Will you call someone?"

"I'll help," she said, stepping down into the gut, where she sank to her knees in soft, black mud. The water was only inches deep.

"Who are you?" she asked, looking at him closely and noting the cuts, the blood, the trailing, twisted arm, and his weakness.

"Does that matter?"

"Yes," she said.

"I'm Flores, site supervisor."

"That's wonderful," she said. "In a way, then, you're responsible. You direct all of it, tell them what to kill?"

He looked at her, beginning to hurt like hell. The salt water was getting to his cuts. The original shock was wearing off and his body was raising hell. "Kill?" He tried to move, and gasped in pain. "What are you talking about?"

"You're the boss?"

"Yeah, listen, I'm beginning to hurt. Will you please go get some of my men?"

"No," she said. "I'm going to watch you die."

He felt cold. There was something about her which scared the hell out of him. He, Jack Flores, was scared of a woman. When he moved, the pain hit him and he went black. When he opened his eyes she was squatting beside him. He figured her as a real nut. She looked it. Her eyes weren't even blinking. They just stared at him. "All right," he said, "tell me what it's all about, huh?"

"I want you to know why you're dying," she said. "I want you to listen, to try to feel. Can you feel it?"

"Huh?" He was listening, all right, and what he heard was good news. He heard a marsh buggy's engine and it was coming closer.

"You should hear it," she said. "The screams. They're dying. Can't you hear it?"

"Yeah, sure," he said, humoring her, waiting as the marsh buggy's engine got louder, definitely coming closer.

But she heard it, too. She stood and looked out over the tall grass. Then she straddled him and pushed his face down into the water. He tried to yell. His face was pushed into the soft mud and he could feel her knees in his back. With her hands she was pushing his face down. He fought, but he was weak. His body bucked and she rode it, hearing the motor coming closer and feeling his muscles spasm. His good arm came up and tried to grasp her legs, but it slid off the muddy fabric of her slacks. She pushed, teeth together, eyes wide, lip pulled back, arms straining. He held his breath, not believing it. He went limp, thinking she'd let him go. His face was pushed into the mud. Water covered his ears. She didn't release him. She pushed harder and he felt the cool, black mud all around his face. He gathered all his strength and bucked and fought, trying to dislodge her. His lungs spasmed. Mud clogged the passages of his nose and filled his mouth and throat. He gagged and then felt the blackness come slowly.

She stood up, waving. The marsh buggy came and stopped. Two men jumped out. "I was standing on the hill," she said, "and I saw him drive into the gut. He was thrown clear. I tried to do something, but he landed in the mud. When I got here he was—" She sobbed.

Jack Flores was in a sitting position. His face was covered with streaks of mud. She had tried to scrape it away, leaving white areas showing through. She'd cleared the mud from his mouth. "I—I tried mouth-to-mouth resuscitation," she said. They could see the mud on her face; they admired her for trying.

The two men loaded Flores onto the marsh buggy. They didn't even notice when she left, looked up to find her gone. The local weekly quoted the two men as saying that an unidentified woman had tried to save the life of the site supervisor. The coroner's verdict was death by suffocation. The mud clogging Jack Flores's nose and throat was too thick to allow water to enter his lungs and drown him.

She washed the black mud away in the clear waters of the pond. It dissipated and drifted to the bottom, to settle lightly on the thick, pulpy plants. She removed her clothes, washed them in the water, and took them inside, washed them again in the machine, dried them, put them back on. She looked fresh. By a coincidence of inspired timing, she heard a whistle down by the pond. She smiled, walked out onto the balcony over the pond. "Up here," she called.

17

What do you do when you think your wife is beginning to crack up? Well, you laugh at yourself and say you're imagining things.

Of course, it was not like Gwen. "I'm glad," she said.

They were discussing the death of Jack Flores. At least George was discussing it. "Boy, what a way to go," he said. "The paper says he must have been alive when he was thrown from the marsh buggy into the mud."

"I'm glad he's dead," Gwen said flatly. It was so unlike her that he could not, at first, credit his ears. "I wish they'd kill all of them," she added with a little smile.

"Honey," he said, "the noise is bad, but that bad?" There was heavy equipment working around the clock. The dredges were a constant, if distant, roar. There were occasional hoots of air horns as the dredgemen signaled. On the island, drag lines were working. They reached their land via a sandy detour. The road next to the beach had been dug away and a small bridge was under construction. It was never quiet. "In another few months we'll have it all to ourselves again. In fact, it'll be more private than ever. There'll only be one way to get here, over the bridge.

There'll be a high wire fence around the canal, so no one will be able just to wander over on our side."

"Yes," she said. It was the only hope she had. She was helpless against the workers in the marsh. "But wouldn't it be divine justice if we could kill all of them?"

"Jesus, you're bloody-minded this morning," he said, kissing her and hurrying off to shave and prepare for work. He thought about it as he shaved. By itself, it could be idle conversation, even if it was desperately out of character for a girl as gentle as Gwen. The pup came in and chewed on his foot, and George jiggled it playfully. When he finished, Gwen was sitting in the big room, hands on the arms of the chair, eyes unblinking, straight ahead. He was shocked, for she was directly in the light of the glass doors and the morning sun and her face looked strained, washed out.

"Do you feel all right?" he asked.

He had to repeat the question. "Oh, sure," she said.

Little things. Her appearance. She was still losing weight. The space between her thighs was back. Her face looked thin. The un-Gwenlike talk about killing. And the house was becoming a botanical garden. Every available inch of sunny window space was occupied by pots containing the flytraps. The demand for insects was so great that George had given up. She fed the flytraps raw hamburger, rationing them to one bit per week. She never seemed to tire of feeding them, dropping the hamburger bits onto the small, black trigger hairs, and watching the trap close. Little things. Her pleasing but rather puzzling reversal in her attitudes toward sex. From a woman who wanted to hide the shameful act under the covers, she'd developed into a wild and wanton sexpot. She liked new things. On Sunday she'd suggested they do it on the lounge on the balcony, in the open air, in broad daylight. Wild, absolutely wild. And then, not once but three or four times, he had come home to find her standing ankle deep in the waters of the clear pond, her head tilted back and her arms hanging limply at her sides. Once he'd seen her swaying in the breeze like a tall sunflower. It was, when you put all the other things together, it was sort of frightening. And that last thing, that was the last straw. The cleared areas were overgrown. He'd gotten out the mower. She, hearing it start, had run out, teased him out it, and taken him inside to distract him. And they'd stayed in bed late that very morning. It was as if she didn't want him to mow the new growth. He was bedamned if he was going to let the damned jungle move back in and take over all of it after all his hard work clearing it.

Little things. Her moodiness. Sometimes he had to speak to her two or three times before she heard. Sometimes she looked at him without recognition in her eyes. And if he didn't know better, he'd have been a suspicious husband because of the innovations she'd introduced into their lovemaking. Once, when she suggested a particularly weird position, he said, "What the hell? Are you experimenting with a kooky lover or something?"

"Reading books, darling," she cooed, urging him into the position, which, he found, was interesting, if rather athletic.

"Gwen, you don't look so good," he said one day. "Why not have Doc Braws check you over?"

"I'm fine," she said.

Then there was the flytrap-gathering expedition. "Honey," he said, when she went off toward the bog with a small trowel and a basket, "those damn things are eating us out of house and home now."

"It'll be cold soon," she said.

"Hell, they're used to the cold. They're tough little beggars. They even live through ground fires."

He followed her, nevertheless. She scooped up only

weak-looking specimens. He tired of it and walked back to the clear pond. He was thinking it might be nice to find some tadpoles somewhere and put them into the pond. The croaking of frogs would, at least, offer a bit of counterpoint to the incessant roar of the heavy equipment. Funny that there weren't frogs there, anyhow. In all his swimming he'd never even seen a minnow. The only life he saw in the pond was the plants and the mosquito larva. He'd been meaning to talk with the game warden and find out about getting some fingerling bass to stock the pond. Be nice to stand on the balcony and cast for a couple of largemouths.

He walked around the pond idly and saw tracks on the far side. Kids were always coming onto the property. He didn't really mind, but he didn't want to think of the little bastards hiding there on the far side of the pond watching them on the balcony. Wow. Here he was the one getting touchy about sex, thinking that they'd better not do it outdoors in the daytime again. Well, what the hell. If she wanted to. Give the little bastards a thrill if they snuck up and saw them. When he was a kid there was this couple in the neighborhood. They got drunk on Saturday afternoons and forgot to close the bedroom shades. A boy could stand in the alley, hidden behind a row of tall okra in the garden, and get an eyeful. He chuckled and turned to see what Gwen was doing. She was on her knees, staring and motionless. She apparently didn't feel his eyes on her. She was about twenty-five yards away. She was close enough for him to see clearly when she cupped her hand in the black, acid earth, lifted it, looked at it thoughtfully, and then took a bite of the dirt. She just lifted her hand, opened her mouth, and took a bite. Just like that.

He didn't mention it to her. When she came up to the house, with several new flytraps to be potted in rich, acid soil, he noticed a smudge on her chin. After that he started watching her more closely. He felt like a spy. He felt disloyal. He wanted to talk it out with her, to say, "Honey, why the hell did you eat dirt?"

Instead, feeling guilty and a bit scared, but not too upset—because she was, after all, his Gwen, and he knew her, and she was probably just going through a stage of nervousness brought on by the constant noise of the heavy equipment—he dropped in on Dr. Irving King the next time he had to go to Port City to the electronics supply house. He let it all hang out, as the expression goes. He talked about her former sexual hangups and the great change, the attachment to the flytraps, her loss of weight, the circles under her eyes, her sleeplessness, and her uncharacteristic remarks about wishing all the construction workers dead.

King seemed to be more interested after that. And when George got around to the dirt eating, he was positively avid for more information, asking questions and waving his cigar, animated. One question was a gasser. "Do you have any reason to suspect that your wife could be, ah, indulging in marital infidelity?" the doctor asked.

George felt anger at first, and then he considered it. "No, none at all. She definitely would not do that."

George talked about the constant noise. King wanted details of the construction project. He got them. He leaned back, puffed on his dead cigar, and then chewed it thoughtfully. "Mr. Ferrier, I think it advisable that you bring your wife in to see me."

"I don't think she'll come," George said. "I've been trying to get her to go in to see our family doctor. She finds a million excuses not to go."

"I see," King said. "You once invited me to visit you."

"Sure," George said.

"I think I will drop in the first of next week."

"Let me know and I'll make it a point to be home," George said.

"I think not," King said. "I'll arrange it to arrive late in the afternoon. Then I can have a chat with Mrs. Ferrier before you come home from work."

"Well," George said, "if that's the way you want it."

When a man is eighty-two, he feels the days growing shorter. The first of the week can mean Monday, Tuesday, or even, in extreme procrastination, Wednesday. But Irving King's curiosity was aroused once more, and when you're eighty-two, if you put things off until Wednesday, Wednesday might never come. He drove to Pine Tree Island on Monday afternoon, arriving at the Ferrier house just after three o'clock. He found it to be a charming place, if a little weedy out front. He walked up the steps to the front deck and looked for a doorbell. There was none. He knocked. Waited. When no one came, he went down the steps carefully and walked around the house. He stood for a long time, with his heart acting up to the point of making him uneasy.

It was not the voyeur in him which caused his agitation. He was too old even for that. It was sheer intellectual excitement, the feeling of finding something. At eighty-two he was being given a second chance, and the coincidence of it was so striking that he had a very good feeling about it all. It was as if some kind god looked down and said, "Irving King, you blew it once. Now here's your second chance."

He could, of course, be aware of the erotic aspect. She was obviously enjoying it. And there was a certain element of perversion, since she and the teen-age boy atop whom she was performing had an audience, another teen-ager who watched as he slowly dressed.

Apparently he had arrived just in time for the last scene of the last act. He could hear her breathing, even from the distance, and then she fell atop the boy and lay still for a moment. The boy, apparently, was ready to go. He pushed her off. She rolled onto the grass and lay there with her eyes closed as the boy quickly pulled on his jeans and shirt. Then she was alone, the two boys having plunged into the thick growth on the far side of the pond. King continued to watch. She rose and walked slowly to the edge of the water, paused, and then plunged in to bathe the sweats and fluids of excess from her body. He waited. She stood, dripping, with her back toward him, her feet planted in shallow water.

"Ah," he said, as she began a slow, steady swaying motion, her arms loose, at her sides, her face tilted heavenwards.

He walked toward her, making no special effort to be quiet. However, she did not hear him. He stood behind her, only feet away. He cleared his throat. She continued to sway slowly.

"Gwen," he said softly. "Gwen."

She turned slowly, without surprise. Her eyes looked into his unblinkingly. "I didn't mean to spy, Gwen," he said.

"You saw then?"

"Yes."

She walked past him and stooped gracefully to pick up her clothing. Her splendidly youthful body was still wet. She slipped into her clothing unhurriedly. "Let's sit on the balcony. You must be tired after your drive."

"A bit," he said, trying to match her coolness. He followed her and sat in a comfortable deck chair. She curled her feet under her on the lounge.

"Would you like to talk about it?" he asked, after a long silence.

"Please don't tell George," she said simply. She was not begging, she was merely making a request.

"Perhaps you will have to tell him. Someday."

"Yes. Someday." She lit a cigarette and blew smoke moodily. "I can't expect you to understand."

"Perhaps I do. A little." He had an eerie feeling of having talked with her, about the same things, before. He drew on that feeling. "It eases the pain."

Her expression told him he'd hit the mark. However, she regained control quickly. "How did you know? You can't feel the pain. We're female. Only we feel it."

Elation mixed with his genuine concern for her. He was the most fortunate of all psychiatrists, to have found two almost identical cases of such great interest. First Evelyn Rogers, in 1937, thinking she could feel the pain of a tree being felled, and then, in his last years, Gwen Ferrier with an identical fantasy.

"But that was why you were, ah, entertaining those lads, wasn't it? So that you could forget the pain, at least for a few moments?"

She nodded.

"Is the pain so terrible?"

She shuddered. "We are so helpless. We can't run. We can only wait, knowing that the pain is coming, that death moves toward us. We anticipate the rending, the tearing, the crushing. We do feel, you know. We have life, feelings, emotions. If you could only know."

"I cannot, of course, actually know without feeling, can I? Human speech isn't the definitive form of communication, is it? I mean, it's so imprecise. Yet, I can understand that you are genuinely disturbed. I find your, uh, communications with the vegetable kingdom to be fascinating, Gwen. Do you mind if I ask you some questions?"

She shrugged.

"Do all plants have awareness?"

"Yes."

"Some more than others?"

She looked at him with narrowed eyes. "Why do you ask?"

"Curiosity. Interest. Concern for you."

"Bullshit." Her unladylike response exploded from her lips. "You don't care. You can't feel."

He glanced at his watch, estimating the time remaining before George arrived. She had to be opened up, but carefully. "But I can understand, at least somewhat. I can believe you." He waited and when she didn't speak he said, "It must be quite terrible to be the only one to feel the pain."

"There are others," she said.

"But not alive." He was taking a shot in the dark.

This gave her pause. She stubbed out her cigarette before looking up, unblinkingly, into his eyes. "Not alive in the sense you understand life."

"Isn't there just one form of life?"

"You see," she said. "You can't possibly understand."

"You say there are others, living in some fashion. I recall another young woman, much like you. She is most certainly dead, by our human standards. She first killed her family."

"She did only what she was forced to do," Gwen said. "She cannot be condemned for doing what she had to do."

It was King's turn to be startled. How much did she know about Evelyn Rogers? How could she know? "You excuse her actions?" he asked, trying to gain time for thought.

"I praise her actions," Gwen said. "She exchanged pain for pain. It was an unequal exchange, true, but she gave terminal pain to six of them."

King felt his ancient heart begin to accelerate. He needed a pill, but he dared not break the mood. "There were only four," he said. "Four loggers. Then her family."

"Six," Gwen said softly. "Two were never found."

"The children," King said. "Did she have to murder her children?" He was stunned, at a loss for words. He had merely assumed that Evelyn Rogers had killed the four loggers. Now this lovely young woman was confirming it, out of a self-confident store of knowledge which caused confusion in his mind, and, moreover, was adding to the grisly score.

"That was sad," Gwen said. "She weeps for them. But she couldn't leave them behind."

"Are they, ah, wherever she is?"

"No." No explanation.

"May I ask," King said, gathering his thoughts, "how you know about her?"

"Evelyn?" The name had not, as yet, been mentioned. "I know."

"You've heard tales?"

"I've heard *the* story," Gwen said, smiling.

"Yes," King said. "She was my patient." That was not what he had wanted to say. He had wanted to ask how Gwen had heard the story.

"Yes," Gwen said. "I know. And I am not your patient, Dr. King."

"Should you be?" he asked, his voice soft and kind.

"For my sake or yours?" She lit another cigarette without haste. "For your sake I stopped seeing you."

"For my sake?"

"We were afraid you'd make the connection."

"But you came to me of your own accord," he said.

"Before I knew Evelyn."

The sun was low. George would be home soon. King had a desperate desire to know, to explore, to probe into her mind. "You can't talk with George about it, for obvious reasons. Wouldn't you like to talk with someone? Would it help if you talked with me?"

She considered. "No," she said. "It would be useless."

"Not to me," he said. "With Evelyn I came close to something, Gwen, something I couldn't understand. We doctors think we know the extent of the human mind. We pride ourselves on being able to take long, extended voyages inside a fellow human's head, but, frankly, we've never gone past the membrane of the brain, except with artificial surgical tools. I'm an old man. I failed to discover whatever it was that made Evelyn Rogers different. I failed to save her." He paused. "I am not necessarily implying that you are in need of salvation, you understand, although some of your actions have certain aspects of self-destruction. Let's just say that I'm burningly curious. For example, I saw you standing in the shallow water. You swayed in the wind. Were you, for that period of time, a plant?" He knew he was being too direct, but time was short.

"No, of course not."

"What then?"

"You wouldn't understand."

"Would you please allow me to try to understand?" He noted her negative reaction and resorted to blackmail. "You don't have a choice, you know. I saw your actions with those two young boys."

She was serene. "That was necessary."

"Would George agree that it was necessary?"

"Yes," she said. "I was afraid it would come to that." She had, in fact, been hoping desperately that he would not push it that far. She sighed. "All right. We'll talk. You will stay for dinner." It was not a question.

"If you like," King said.

"Depending on which sources you read," Gwen said, "the Germans killed three to seven million Jews during World War II. Imagine, if you can, being there, being able to see it all, and, more importantly, being able to feel it all. Multiply hopeless death, terror, agony by seven million."

"I'll admit openly that I can't imagine it," King said. "The mind is peculiar that way. We just cannot accept mass death. The death of one man, closely observed, is more moving than the extermination of millions."

"But if you could feel a million deaths."

"Can you?"

"We share all," she said.

"We?"

"Yes, we. We plants. All of us."

"All trees? All weeds?" He removed a cigar from his pocket and began to unwrap it. He chewed the end of it thoughtfully. When she remained silent he asked, "Why are you the only one to communicate with them?"

"I told you there have been others."

"Evelyn? Who else?"

"A girl. She's here, too."

"Where?"

"There," Gwen said, looking toward the center of the clear, green waters of the pond. "She drowned there."

"And she's there now?"

"Yes, with Evelyn. With them."

"As I remember it, now that you've mentioned it, she drowned with her boyfriend. Is he there?"

"We are female," she said.

"Males can't feel or communicate?"

"We are female."

"All plants?" King asked.

"No, of course not. Us."

"I see," he said, not seeing at all. "When you say, we are female, you are talking about some special sort of plant. You are not referring to you, Evelyn, and the other girl, or to plants in general, only something special."

She rose. "Will you walk with me?"

He followed her into the boggy area at the lower end of the pond. As they crossed toward high ground she said, "Don't step on them. Watch out for them." He saw the flytraps. They were almost hidden under taller weeds and grasses. He stepped carefully.

"Are the flytraps the special ones?" he asked.

She smiled. "That's almost funny." She led the way to the high ground on the far side of the pond. There mushrooms grew. She selected, bent, and plucked them.

"Mushrooms don't feel, then," King said, pleased to catch her in an inconsistency.

"Fungi are poor, dumb things, not truly alive."

"I see. But back to the flytraps."

"Yes. There is a certain ironic humor in what they are called." She was selecting more mushrooms. "You call them Venus-flytraps, as if they were not of this earth."

"They're not?"

"It was a miracle that they survived," she said. She had picked a half-dozen mushrooms. Her hands full, she passed the mushrooms on to King. He held them gingerly. They were clammy and slick in his hand. "The crash burned everything, everything except for a few small root portions which were thrown clear."

"Ah," King said. "I think I have it. There was a crash. A spaceship? And the flytraps, an alien species, survived."

"Yes."

"Then they're the special ones. When you refer to us, or we, you're talking about you and the flytraps." Actually, it made a special sort of sense. Disordered minds often built quite credible fantasies.

"They're only plants," she said.

"Then I'm confused again," King admitted. He accepted another handful of mushrooms. "I take it we're eating these?"

"Yes."

"I usually get them from a can."

"They're quite safe." She smiled at him. "Believe me, I know."

"Yes, I suppose you would know." He followed her back across the bog, stepping gingerly. "May I ask who are the special ones?"

"I'm going to ask you to use your imagination again," she said. "Imagine a world where death is unknown."

"And, again, you're asking for something very difficult, especially for a man of eighty-two who faces death daily."

"I'm talking about immortality for every living thing."

"But isn't that impossible? Don't big fishes eat little fishes on your world?"

"On our world everything we need is here." She stooped and lifted a handful of dirt.

"Then they're all plants on that world."

"In a way. Oh, they can move. They are intelligent. They are, in fact, far ahead of us. They came here in a great ship, across vast distances. They carried their own earth with them. They returned to it for rest and sustenance, remembering all the while the beauty of the home world, longing to return, but curious about the universe. Think of the shock to them to discover death. In their world there was only life. No living thing ate any other living thing. It was the earth which provided, earth, the eternal earth which fed and sustained and kept. And, in return, they nourished the earth with their bodies."

"Ah," King said. "Without dying?"

"Think of a wheat field. You may believe that a wheat field dies on maturity. It does not. The life force is stored in the seeds. On the home world it is much the same. There were new beginnings for the body, but the life force was a constant. Life, itself, went on, learning, loving beauty, and living in eternal peace. Then they came here."

"To crash and die," King said. They were at the steps to the balcony. He panted slightly as he climbed.

"Their bodies died," she explained. "And most of their specimens. Only one of the plants aboard survived and adapted. At home, the plants did not have to eat insects." She led the way into the kitchen, took the mushrooms from his hands, and put them into the sink for washing.

He sat down at the dining table as she began to prepare the meal. "The life force managed to transfer. At first, it lived in sort of a limbo, rootless. Then water collected in the crater caused by the crash. Native waterplants took root. One was adaptable. It was a poor substitute for what we had known, but it provided a body, a stationary body, a prison. There was no escape. It was so lonely, and there was death all around. There was wildfire and animals nibbling leaves. Our plants are not as highly developed as theirs, but they still are living beings and can feel pain and know death. Death was a new and terrible experience. We—they concentrated together in the crater. The flytraps, lower on the life scale and more adaptable, spread over a small area, the area they now inhabit. It was good to have the flytraps. They represented something known in a strange and terrible world. Through the flytraps they can leave the pond, widen their horizon, experience something other than sameness. But they don't like it out here. Mostly they stay in the pond, where they've forced out all of the native life forms. This, we feel, is selfish, but necessary. A turtle eating a water plant is sheer torture."

"So the special beings are in the pond," King said. He was amazed by the clarity of her account and astounded by the grandness of her delusion. He was secretly pleased by the uniqueness of her madness.

"They didn't want me to tell you. They've killed in the past to keep their secret."

"And to stop the pain?"

"Yes."

"But if there is an alien intelligence living in the pond, why not make itself known, since it has you as a spokesman?"

She laughed. "Are you saying, Dr. King, that you believe me?"

He had to laugh with her. "I see your point."

"There is the problem of communication. It is largely a one-way thing, more an influence than something expressed. They can make themselves known to me—"

"Just to you?"

"To a chosen female of any species." She paused. She was past the point of no return. "And, in special cases, to certain others. There was my cat, Satan. Before he came to me someone had denatured him. He was a neuter, a nothing. They reached Satan and used him to keep me from killing myself."

"I would not lose much, at my age, by being a eunuch," King said with a crinkly smile. "Would they talk to me?" He realized quickly that his attempt at levity had fallen short. "So they speak to females only?"

"They influence, make known the core of themselves, they share. In return, they receive mainly emotions, strong emotions. They recognize intent, intent to do harm or to do good."

"An ability and talent shared by plants in general?"

"To a limited extent."

"And they can control your actions?"

"Not control," she said. "They can only show, share, and appeal. That, of course, is a strong influence, for it is very dramatic to be able to share the death of a thousand living beings. Who would be unaffected? Who would not respond?"

"As you have responded?" King asked.

"Yes."

"May I ask why you're telling me this now?"

"I need time," she said, turning from her cooking to look at him. "Soon the deaths will end, at least for now. Then we'll have peace again. We've known this all along. We know we should not act, call attention to ourselves, but the pain, in such masses, such waves, is maddening, unbearable. We've been forced to do things—"

He broke the silence which followed. "Such as the intimate activities with the young boys? Let me see if I understand. Sex is a vividly strong emotion. You share that emotion with those who feel the pain, thus blacking out the pain for a moment."

"Yes."

He phrased his next question carefully. "When Evelyn Rogers was alive the island was being timbered. Thus, from what you've told me, there was pain as the trees were cut. Was she helping them, the ones in the pond, by engaging in sex acts? Was she extracting a measure of revenge when she killed the loggers?"

"She had to. Can't you see? There was no other way. You can't just do nothing when mass murder is being performed. You have to do something."

"I must ask this, Gwen," he said. "Have you done anything other than engage in sex to help them?"

She turned to look at him. She smiled. "Do I look like a killer?"

He had to admit she did not. At the moment, she looked like a typical young housewife busy with her meal. She looked attractive, neat, and charming. But then so had Evelyn Rogers.

"That must not happen, Gwen."

She turned away.

"Will you come to my office regularly until the, ah, pain is over?"

"Is that the deal?" she asked.

"Call it that if you like," he said. "I'd prefer you call it concern for you."

"All right."

He hesitated, but curiosity was hot in him. "Would it be possible for me to have a sample of the plants of the pond, the plants which are inhabited by this alien life force?"

She turned to look at him with unblinking eyes. "If you should try to disturb them I'd have to kill you."

King felt his chest tighten, but the entry of George precluded an immediate answer or further questioning.

18

"Hey, we're going to be notorious," George said, after greeting Dr. King. King had no way of knowing that George's next statement was, for the good doctor, a death sentence. "Some kids found a body up by the canal cut today."

King looked quickly toward Gwen, his mind rebelling at the thought. She showed only proper interest.

It was the young kid who had wanted to earn an extra dollar by working overtime. She'd killed him badly. He was still alive when she had tumbled him into the hole and, in his terminal agony, his movements had disturbed the thin layer of sand and leaves atop him. The diggings of small, carrion-eating animals had further uncovered him. The stench, thus freed of the covering earth, had led Gwen's two late afternoon playmates, the brothers Don and Tommy Promer, to the sunken hole. The sight of the kid's rotting skull, gnawed by rodents, mutilated by the shotgun blast, had an effect on the boys which would not fade quickly.

And it was not 1937. The kid was not Negro. When Don and Tommy reported their find, after a headlong race to the island police station, things began to move rapidly. Even as Gwen Ferrier prepared club steaks, rare, topped with native mushrooms, the search was still going on up in the woods. Before Dr. Irving King died, there would be other grisly discoveries, but he would not know.

She was calm. She knew what she had to do. It was relatively simple. While George and Dr. King sat in the big room with cigars and a pre-dinner drink, she slipped out the back door and walked in the light of a rising moon, plucked the poison mushrooms and spiced one steak with them.

Mushroom poisoning can vary with the individual. Some of the more deadly varieties, such as the milky-white destroying angel, are fatal in about fifty percent of reported cases. Other varieties can produce anything from death to mild stomach upset. Gwen had only the fly amanita close at hand. It had one advantage over the more deadly species. Its effects were almost immediate.

She served a nice little Spanish wine with the steaks. George wanted to talk about the discovery of the decomposing body. She forbade it. "Honey," she protested, "I want to enjoy my dinner."

She made her announcement toward the end of the meal, after George had hungrily demolished his food. Dr. King was eating slowly, mixing the meat taste with the plentiful supply of mushrooms on his plate. "Dr. King thinks I should go into therapy."

"Well," George said, "he's the doctor."

It was a pleasant meal. She was, for a change, ravenous. She finished her steak and salad, even most of the baked potato. They talked about the peculiarities of the flytraps over an after-dinner glass of wine. Dr. King began to show some agitation within fifteen minutes.

"Anything wrong, doc?" George asked.

"Nothing, nothing," King said, wiping his eyes, his glasses held in his hand.

"I've been thinking," George said: "It's a long drive back to Port City and we've got an extra bed."

"Very kind of you," King said, shaking his head. "I suppose it's just the excitement of the trip."

"Come in the living room and sit down," Gwen said, rising.

"Yes, yes." He stumbled as he rose, and caught himself on the edge of the table. "Perhaps, because the food was so delicious, I overdid it a bit."

Gwen took his arm and guided him to a comfortable chair. "Is there anything I can do?"

"No, I'm sure I'll be all right in a moment."

George looked at Gwen with a raised eyebrow. "I seem to be having trouble with my eyes," King said in a matter-of-fact voice. George, feeling helpless, bent and looked into King's eyes. Gwen did not have to bend to see that his pupils were dilated.

"Would you like to lie down?" she asked.

"Yes, I think so."

Together they helped him to the guest bedroom. He lay down after Gwen removed his jacket and loosened his tie. He began to take his own pulse. "Hummm," he said. "I wonder, George, if you'd go out and get my bag. You'll find it in the trunk of the car."

"Sure," George said. When he came back, King was breathing rapidly and rubbing his eyes. "Here we go, doc," he said.

"I'm afraid I can't see too well," King said. "But there's a small bottle with small blue pills in the side pocket." Gwen brought water. King was twitching as if in excitement, his pupils huge. "Don't let me worry you," he said. "Please go ahead and relax. It's just the stomach of an old man protesting too many good things."

"You're sure you're all right?" George said. "I can call Dr. Braws."

"No, no," King said. "No need for that."

"You go ahead, George," Gwen said. "I'll stay with him."

"Well, O.K.," George said, feeling uncomfortable and unable to help.

She closed the door behind him and sat beside the bed,

her hands folded. King muttered to himself. "Agitation, spells of near blindness, rapid pulse."

"You'll be all right," Gwen said.

"Drug," he muttered, trying to sit up. "A drug."

"No," she said, leaping up to push him back. "Just lie still."

The hallucinations began shortly. She could hear George making himself useful, clinking plates as he loaded the dishwasher. The sound came to her dimly, backgrounded, eternally, by the distant roar of the heavy equipment.

"Ruth," King said, looking at her with wide eyes. "You're so beautiful, Ruth."

"Yes," she whispered.

"Your left breast is larger than the right," he said, reaching. She did not move as his hand smoothed her knit blouse, cupped. "Such lovely breasts, Ruth."

"Yes," she whispered.

"May I see them?"

"Yes." She lifted her blouse. As usual, she was bare. She sat on the side of the bed, letting his hand fondle her.

"Isn't it beautiful?" he asked, removing his hand, pointing. "Can you imagine it, Ruth, as it was, with people, alive, complete?"

"Yes," she said.

"Pericles said let it be, and it is," he said, his eyes looking into a distance. "For us, Ruth. Once it held Athena in gold and ivory. See it?"

"I see it," she said.

"And no strong Greek boys to carry us," he said. "We can soar, Ruth. Soar! Come with me."

"Yes, I'll come," she said, pushing her blouse down to cover her nakedness.

He extended his arms. "Come," he said, his eyes wide and unseeing. Visions were replacing vision.

She went into his arms, laying the pillow over his face and putting her weight on him. She felt his old arms around her, weak. He struggled only briefly. She pressed her cheek against the pillow, lying full-length atop him and feeling the last spasms of his lungs.

"George," she said, white-faced, tears on her cheeks. "He—he just stopped breathing."

19

In one respect, at least, Ocean County had not changed since 1937. Good people did not automatically suspect other good people of murder. Not only did those good people, among them Dr. Peter Braws, not suspect, but the possibility did not even enter their minds. Therefore, no autopsy was performed on the remains of Dr. Irving King, late of Port City, the psychiatrist who came to dinner and stayed to die.

Good people said, "How terrible it must have been for that nice young couple."

Ruth Henley sat at King's desk and wept. Her aged shoulders heaved for a few moments, and her faded eyes bled tears uncolored by mascara. Then she rose and began the task of destroying the doctor's files. If, in the process of sorting and packing for the incinerator thirty-five years of a man's work, she felt that she was also preparing to burn away that many years of her own life, she gave no outward sign. It was only when she found a copy of the doctor's will in his desk, with a short note attached, that she wept again. By that time the workmen hired to burn the records had gone. The note said, "Ruthie, go to Greece." The contents of the will made it possible.

The funeral was attended by a large mass of people, among them the nice young couple in whose home the doctor had suffered his fatal cardiac seizure. Gwen cried. George wiped his eyes.

Then it was over.

There was only the daily mutter of the heavy equipment, the hooting of the dredge airhorns. There were only the few more weeks of pain to endure, and then, and then. . . .

And then Cowboy Gore, old, equipped with the mind of a boy, attracted by the search activity which had turned up two bodies in one hole, still another in a separate hole, stumbled upon the shallow water. Cowboy's memory was a clouded uncertainty, but there were things which were strong. She was one of those things. He stood watching. She was dressed in one of those tiny bathing suits and it made Cowboy's old body seem young again, and he whistled. It was automatic, that whistle. It was a one-toned blast of sound which came from between his teeth and rang out over the pond to turn Gwen's head and to attract the attention of George, reading on the balcony. Gwen looked, saw the hat, the old face, and was puzzled. She had told them, all of them, never, never to come to the house on the weekend. But then she was relieved, because she didn't know the man who stood on the other side of the pond. He whistled again and waved. She turned and looked up at George.

"Who is it?" he asked.

"I don't know," she said.

George put down his book and came down the stairs. When Cowboy saw him he bolted, crashing through the brush with all the grace and quietness of a stampeded elephant. George laughed. "Jesus, am I that frightening?"

"You don't scare me at all," Gwen said.

"I've been meaning to do something about that," George said.

She held her breath. What did he mean?

"I saw tracks over there the other day." He grinned. "I'm afraid, my shy and bashful wife, that our open-air exhibitions may have had, at one time or more, an audience."

"Oh, no," she gasped.

It was a torrid and humid August afternoon, but he'd been putting on weight lately. He went in, dressed for the job in boots and work clothes, came out equipped with ax, saw, and determination.

"Don't, George," she said, following him toward the far side of the pond. "I like it that way. It's so natural."

"I'll just clear away the close stuff, right next to the pond. Then the little bastards won't have a place to hide."

"George, please don't?" He looked at her, concerned by the pleading tone. "Let's just—"

"It needs to be done," he said. "I've been intending to do it."

"George—" What could she say? She couldn't tell him it would hurt. She had already concluded that Dr. King's visit had not been accidental or coincidental. It had followed too closely upon George's last visit to Port City. So he was already half-convinced that she needed professional help. To tell him the truth would, she knew, confirm his suspicion.

"I'll need a brush stacker and burner," George said. "Know anyone who's interested in the job?"

"No," she said curtly, leaving him and running toward the house.

He moved to follow, and then decided against it. This nuttiness about plants had to end sometime. Hell, he couldn't even mow the lawn or clear the trees—rather, the small oak seedlings which had sprouted in his cleared areas. It was too much. He went to work, taking out his momentary unhappiness on the passive small growth. He had to take breaks frequently until he was soaked, and nature's air conditioning system began functioning, sweat cooling as it evaporated. Then it was a rhythmic swing and pull as muscles loosened, and his body felt alive, healthy. He cleared a ring in which to pile the brush, then worked on the margin of the pond. Gwen did not come out. It soon became a contest of wills. He would work, cut brush, until she came out. In the end, she won. After two hours of it—hot, tired, sweaty, a huge pile of brush ready for burning, the visible result of his labor, a cleared swath alongside the pond—he stood, bent his aching back with one hand on his hip, and looked at the lowering sun.

He carried the ax and saw toward the house. The pond was green, clear and cool-looking. He put the ax and saw on the grass, stripped off his sweat-soaked clothing, and cooled himself. Refreshed, he sat in the shallow water and bellowed for Gwen. She was still playing coy, refusing to answer, did not show herself. He grinned. He'd show her. He was not going in until she came out.

But it was boring to sit in the shallow water with the pulpy green things wiggling against his legs when he moved. There was another project he'd been neglecting, one which could be accomplished in the cool of the pond. He went to the garage, got hoe and rake, and attacked the water plants in his swimming area, cutting them below sand with the hoe and raking them out with the rake. They were tough, surprisingly tough, but he was strong, and his energies had been restored. A pile of the green stuff grew rapidly. He halted for a brief rest. White sand was beginning to show and he would have a nice little beach and a clear bottom area soon. Then he looked at the pile of green stuff.

"Jesus Christ," he said under his breath. The stuff was alive. It writhed. It moved. It crawled. He'd never seen anything like it. It acted almost as if it were trying to crawl back to the water, but the effect was like looking into a bucket of green worms. "Jesus," he repeated, cutting one of the wriggling pieces with his hoe. The severed parts continued to writhe.

At first she was dreaming. She'd thrown herself across the bed, bathing suit damp. Strangely, the clearing operation did not affect her, save for a dull, sharp, dull, sharp, rather minor pain. It was nothing compared with the mass destruction of the marsh, and the giant agonies of hundred-year-old oaks. It was, she concluded, a price they would have to pay. She was even able to doze through it, wishing he'd stop, but unable to come up with a solution which would serve to stop him without making him think she was going crazy. He would tire. He would stop. It wouldn't last for weeks, months, as the huge pain had lasted. It was bearable.

But this. It devastated her; this dream was more horrible, more dreadful, and more painful than anything that had been done to them before. It was the ultimate horror, the nightmare which had been feared for hundreds of thousands of years. It was so terrible she couldn't scream, could only writhe on the bed, a sensitive being in an agony which wouldn't stop, couldn't be conquered, even temporarily, by fainting.

Then it wasn't a dream. It was happening. She tried to scream out, beg it to stop. Her muscles spasmed, drew her into a knot. She fought. "Stop it, stop it," her mind screamed, every cell on fire, every nerve tortured. She struggled to the glass doors leading onto the balcony, saw him working again, killing, maiming, striking at the central sanctuary. "Oh, God, no," she thought, still unable to scream.

Pain jerked her to the bare boards as she struggled onto the balcony and it left her weak. She pushed herself up, held to the railing for support, made it down the stairs, her mouth working, eyes wide, streaming tears, body jerking with the horrible pain.

"No, no, stop." It was soundless. He wouldn't even turn around. She fell and writhed on the grass.

George had lost his awe. Hell, they were just plants. There were millions of them in the pond. What if he did cut out a few? They were eerie things, funny. He wouldn't have been a bit surprised to find that they had something to do with the complete lack of life in the pond, no fish, no frogs. If they did, indeed, as he thought, help keep the water clear, then he'd keep them. He'd rather have a clear, clean swimming place than a muddy frog and fish pond, but it wouldn't hurt at all to expose some wading sand near the bank. Then maybe Gwen would swim with him.

He was working in calf-deep water, reaching out in front and dragging cut weeds towards him; he was getting ready to turn and stack the cut weeds onto the pile on the bank when the ax blade cut into his leg behind the knee, severing tendons and slicing through the joint to leave his left leg dangling by the tissue surrounding the kneecap. He fell backward with a splash, blood spurting. The second blow severed his right arm at the elbow. There was no pain, only the awareness of a heavy blow, but his eyes saw and knew, and he screamed hoarsely, a sound of ultimate terror, the sound of knowledge. His arm was gone, his leg gushing blood. The irreparable had been done, and he screamed his disbelief.

"Gwen?" he said, his voice trailing into another scream as the ax, bloody, sharp, and deadly, narrowly missed his left wrist and lopped four fingers off at the second joint.

Then he was crawling for his life, leg dangled, his arm gone, blood darkening the water. Gwen, his Gwen. Her fourth blow was weaker, the pain still there, but the initial strength of adrenal action gone. The blow laid open the calf of his good leg and glanced off the bone; but there were other blows as he moved more slowly, his eyes blurring and his life's blood swirling out in arterial gushes into the clear pond.

She continued to chop, breathing in sobbing agony. The strap to her bikini top had broken. The small scrap of material hung from her neck, flapping with her movements. Water and perspiration and blood beaded her lower legs.

When it was over, when she had, with cold, logical reasoning stopped her hysterical sorrow, she worked steadily. First things first. First, all the water plants were carefully placed back in the sand, planted lovingly. Then the pain was eased.

George lay face up in shallow water. And toes up in shallow water. And fingers up in shallow water. And in small bits of finger in shallow water. And it was over. The dark clouds of blood released into the greenness were being dissipated and absorbed. To avoid dripping blood, however, she went to the house for large towels. He was quite heavy. One light tap with the ax on the almost severed leg lightened the load.

She placed him, in some approximation of order, in their bed, and stood looking down at him. "I am so damn sorry, darling," she said. His open eyes screamed at her accusingly. She closed them. They didn't want to stay closed.

She checked the pond again and washed the sands of the edge with water cupped into her hands. She stored the ax and saw in the garage. It was rapidly growing late; the sun was almost down. She crawled in the shallow water, moving her hands, stirring the settled blood and swirling it away.

"It's time, isn't it?" she asked, standing ankle deep in the water, the pulpy, green, replanted things caressing her bare feet and ankles.

She drove the M.G. into the garage beside the pick-up

and closed the door. There was a full five-gallon can of gasoline for the power mower. She struggled into the house with it, doused the living room rug, went into the bedroom, and poured the rest on George. When she threw a match into the living room from the deck, the resultant whoosh singed her hair and pushed her back with a blast of heat.

She stood in the water, ankle deep, and watched. When the fire topped out, the ceilings and roof falling in a towering storm of sparks and flame, she had to go deeper. From there, just her head out of the water, hair floating on the clear green, she stayed and watched until she heard the vehicles coming up the road.

"Now," she said. "Now."

She submerged, swam underwater, deep, deeper, to the center of the pond, lungs beginning to ache, stars exploding before her open eyes. There was no light, but the darkness was friendly, familiar. In the deepest part, she reached down, found them, clasped them in her hands, and pulled herself down among them. Her body was buoyant and wanted to rise, but she clung, worked her arms, her feet, her legs down among the tangled, pulpy, cool water plants. They caressed her cheeks. They soothed her body. She was still wearing the bikini, bottom in place, halter loose. "Now," she thought, and it was so beautiful that she wanted to cry. She exhaled. Bubbles erupted at the surface, unseen; She inhaled. Her body, no longer made light by the air it contained, settled slowly into the soft, thick growth.

"Why," she thought, "it's like going to sleep."

20

"What you got here," the real estate man said, "is your own little island. One road in. The canal cutting you off from the rest. Big high fence along the canal so that no one can get in without coming up the road. Ideal for privacy."

"Mighty poor soil," sighed the prospective buyer, his hand full of sand. He let it trickle drily through his fingers. "I'd have to have it tested."

"Frankly," said the real estate man, "I don't know what kind of soil you need to grow grapes, but I know this. There isn't another plot of land this size for sale in the whole county, and if it weren't for the power company canal, this plot would be prime residential property and you couldn't touch it for twice the price. Hell, you couldn't touch it for four times the price. Then, too, you got this situation. The fellow owned it had no close relatives, just a cousin or something out in California, some kind of hippy interested in the quick buck. You put it off too long and he might decide to come out here and look at it and go up on the price."

"I'd have to have the soil checked," the prospective buyer said. "And then I'd have to check the cost of clearing it. I'd need about all of it cleared, at least the central hundred acres."

"No sweat there," the real estate man said, checking over his shoulder to see where the woman had wandered off to. He didn't want her over by the pond. The bush was taking the burned house site, but it was still raw and rough and there was no use spooking her by reminding her of the ill luck of former owners. Women were spooky enough anyhow. She was moving down toward the creek. "It's just scrub oak and loblolly. Good dozer operator can have a hundred acres whipped out in a week or so."

"Well, it *looks* like good grape soil," the prospective buyer said. He squatted and scooped up sand into a plastic bag. He had it half full when the woman screamed.

"Oh, shit," the real estate man said, "what now?"

He broke into a run and pushed through the growth. The woman was standing against a great oak tree and was cornered by a goddamned alligator, of all things. A frigging alligator. It was just a small alligator, being a North Carolina alligator and not having much warm weather for growing time. But it was a belligerent little bastard, and it was advancing with its mouth wide, making a hissing sound.

Last time it had been a goddamned rattlesnake, and it had bit the stupid woman, and he'd had to suck blood and venom out after cutting her leg with a pocketknife. Before that a goddamned fox, acting just as crazy as that time with the Ferrier woman and that goddamned possum. What kind of a frigging zoo was this?

He scared the alligator off.

The prospective buyer called the next day. "We've decided that the acreage you were showing us won't do," he said.

"You'll never find anything at such a bargain," the real estate man said.

"Well, we'd have to live there, too, you know. And the little woman didn't take to the place."

"No," the real estate man said. "I didn't think she would."

He hung up, sighing. Two hundred three and a quarter acres of prime development land fouled up by a goddamned radioactive canal and you couldn't even sell it at giveaway prices for some fool to plant grapes on. But there was one thing. They weren't making any more land. Sooner or later he'd sell it again. Maybe one of the locals would get over being superstitious and take a flyer. He didn't care who bought it and he didn't care what they did with it. He didn't care how many bodies they'd dug up on it, or how many houses had burned down, or how many people had drowned in the clear pond. They just weren't making any more land, and sooner or later. . . . *Humm, ten percent of—*

HUNGRY FOR MORE?

Learn about the Twisted History of '70s and '80s Horror Fiction

---

"Pure, demented delight."
—*The New York Times Book Review*

Take a tour through the horror paperback novels of two iconic decades . . . if you dare. Page through dozens and dozens of amazing book covers featuring well-dressed skeletons, evil dolls, and knife-wielding killer crabs! Read shocking plot summaries that invoke devil worship, satanic children, and haunted real estate! Horror author and vintage paperback book collector Grady Hendrix offers killer commentary and witty insight on these trashy thrillers that tried so hard to be the next *Exorcist* or *Rosemary's Baby*.

AVAILABLE WHEREVER BOOKS ARE SOLD.

Visit QuirkBooks.com for more information about this book and other titles by Grady Hendrix.

QUIRK BOOKS